SATAN'S DAUGHTERS

SATAN'S DAUGHTERS

George G. Gilman

NEW ENGLISH LIBRARY/TIMES MIRROR

For:
Joan and Alan,
the friendliest
bartenders in town!

A New English Library Original
Publication, 1978
© by George G. Gilman, 1978

First NEL paperback edition August 1978

NEL Books are published by
New English Library Limited from
Barnard's Inn, Holborn,
London EC1N 2JR
Made and printed in Great Britain by
Hunt Barnard Printing Ltd.,
Aylesbury, Bucks

45003717 7

Chapter One

The horse smelled its own kind and vented a low, nervous snort. The man detected a faint trace of woodsmoke and reacted with a soft sigh. The black gelding pricked up his ears but the rider made no other sound. The silence of an untroubled night draped them again, disturbed only by the monotonous clop of shod hooves against the hard-packed earth of west Texas as mount and man continued to move along the bank of the arroyo at the same easy pace as before.

The gelding was immediately calm, totally trusting of the man. The man appeared to be as wearily nonchalant as before, but behind the veneer of composure he had become instantly tense. His sense of smell had told him that a fire was burning nearby and now his eyes concentrated their steady gaze on the line of low, smooth-contoured hills which crossed his path a quarter mile ahead: seeking a glow of flame or a column of smoke. Experience warned him to expect trouble. For his name was Adam Steele.

Habit insisted that he take from a pocket of his suit jacket a pair of black buckskin gloves and draw them on. And he rode then with the reins held in his left hand, while his right rested loosely on his thigh – six inches from where the stock of a Colt Hartford revolving rifle jutted from its boot.

Anyone who saw this would not have drawn any uneasy

conclusions from the rider's actions. For there was an unhurried carelessness about the way the man moved.

As Sunday became Monday the Texas night grew colder so the man donned a pair of gloves. And the movement of the hand from the reins to the leg? A rider who had been many hours in the saddle was inclined to be restless.

Then there was the general appearance of the man, which offered few clues to the breed he truly was. He was small of stature — perhaps a half inch taller than five feet six, and his frame was lean. About thirty-five years of age. He was not handsome and yet neither was he homely. His features were as lean and regular as his build, dominated by coal black eyes and flanked by long sideburns of prematurely grey hair. His mouthline might have suggested gentleness or even weakness had it not been for the hard, pebble-like quality of his eyes and the deeply scored texture of his complexion.

His mode of dress was a mixture of city and country styles. For he wore a well-tailored grey suit with blue stitching, a purple vest and a white shirt trimmed with lace at the front, fancy brown and white riding boots, a workaday grey Stetson and a grey silk kerchief which hung loosely around his neck. All these items had seen better days and were stained, torn and scuffed from more than one day's easy riding across the southern end of the Llano Estacado.

He wore no gunbelt and his only visible weapon was the sporting rifle in the boot hung forward of his right leg. It would have needed a very keen observer to spot that the split seam in the outside of his right pants leg gave access to a wooden-handled knife stored in a boot sheath: or that weighted corners of his kerchief made the simple square of silk an instrument of strangulation.

He held the gelding on the arroyo bank as the course of the dried-up stream bed curved into the low hills which marked the border between the state of Texas and territory of New Mexico. The smell of burning wood was stronger now, but still he saw no smoke or flame. A horse snickered to give him a bearing and he tugged gently on the reins to veer his gelding to the left. He did not touch his unspurred heels to the flanks of his mount and was carried up the grassy knoll at the same easy pace as before. But the travel-weary animal had to work harder on the incline and the expelled breath of exertion showed as white vapour at the flared nostrils. The tough and dusty grass muted the sounds of the hooves as they were set down.

Trusting his experience-honed sixth sense for danger, which on this night failed to trigger a warning that he was being watched, Steele did not rein his mount to a halt until he reached the crest of the hill. And was skylined against a cloudless infinity sprinkled with diamond-bright stars and lit by the hard glow of a threequarter moon.

As he reached his vantage point he was in time to see the final ember of a fire fade into the greyness of wood ash. But the highly placed moon provided ample light for him to survey the night camp set up in the broad hollow among encircling hills.

To the left, fifty feet down and away from him, four horses were hobbled and tied together by long lengths of rope. The animals were resting easy now that they had seen the gelding and rider on the hilltop above them.

Resting even easier – blissfully unaware of the watching intruder – were the seven people who slept beneath warm blankets on the other side of the dead fire from the horses.

Beyond where the seven slept a Concord coach was parked: heavily laden with equipment and supplies for a long trip, dusty from recent travel and marked by the scars of past neglect.

Steele took in the component parts of the night camp at a single glance and then surveyed the bedded-down forms more carefully. He reached a conclusion about them, vented a soft grunt of surprise, did a double take to confirm his findings – and grinned. It was an expression which contrasted with the premature greyness of his hair, seeming to cause him to shed many years because of the boyishness it gave his weather-bronzed face.

All seven who slept so peacefully in the hollow below him were women.

The grin remained on his bristled face as he clucked his horse forward, steering the gelding down into the hollow. As he rode he took off the buckskin gloves but did not taunt himself for having instinctively donned them beside the arroyo. Because for many years – a whole lifetime in terms of the man he had become under the forging influence of violence – his survival had depended upon his constant readiness to meet danger at every turn. The stained and torn gloves were a symbol of this darkest side of the man's character: and if he could pull them off his hands without experiencing evil or violence there was never any feeling of inanity. Such occasions were infrequent and he felt a brief sense of gratitude.

But because a man had escaped death countless times in as many places, this did not make him faultless. And as he neared the foot of the slope, with both hands in control of the reins again, he made the mistake of blotting out memories of recent events which sought to flood his mind. Vivid recollections of the widows of Borderville, of a rich girl and a whore in New Orleans, and of the oddly assorted trio of women who had played their different roles to trigger the slaughter which came to the ghost town of Rain.

All of them were in the past now and should be forgotten. But that was a luxury denied Adam Steele, or indulged in at his peril. The memories beat at the mental barrier he had raised against them and he scowled out of the grin as the gelding reached the flat floor of the hollow: resenting that he had learned so well the primary lesson in the art of survival on the narrow line between life and death – that a man must prejudge the future in the light of what has happened in the past, until the present is proved to hold no threat.

'Move a muscle and I'll blow your teeth out through the back of your head!'

The gelding swung his head towards the source of the spite-filled voice. Steele moved only his eyes in their sockets. And the scowl of rancour remained fixed on his features for a moment longer. Then he became impassive as one woman folded up into a sitting posture and the others jolted awake with grunts, moans and husky words of complaint.

'I usually tip my hat to ladies, ma'am,' he answered evenly in his distinctive Virginia drawl. But he made no move to do so.

For the woman who was now sitting rigidly ten feet away from him had snatched a Winchester rifle from beneath her

8

blanket and angled it directly up at him. Her aim was rock steady.

'Try it and Saint Peter'll be the only one you impress, mister. Or the devil if you ain't lived right.'

His hands, still holding the reins as they draped the saddlehorn, did not move. But he did swing his head from side to side now, spreading the boyish grin back across his face as he looked at each woman in turn.

'If it wasn't for the guns, ma'am, a man might think he'd just ridden into a little piece of heaven right here on earth.'

The woman with the Winchester was about sixty and very fat. With bleached blonde hair tightly rolled in curlers. She had a fleshy face with bulbous cheeks that squeezed her eyes to narrow lines of glittering anger and crowded her large nose. The age wrinkles around her eyes and broad mouth all had a downward turn so that her leathery features seemed incapable of ever showing a smile.

'Kill him, Mrs Lucifer! My Pa sent him! Kill him!'

All the other women provided a pleasant contrast to the old one's ugliness. But the girl who spat out the shrill imprecation was the prettiest of all. And the youngest. She was no more than eighteen with a turned up nose, small mouth and large eyes which gave her face an elfin quality under the fringe of her straight, short-cut brown hair. Fear bordering on terror was plain to see in every line of her pale features. The Army Colt which she aimed waveringly at Steele in a double-handed grip was not cocked.

'Mrs Lucifer?' Steele posed with surprise as he glanced at all the women again and then fixed his attention on the one with the Winchester.

Between the youngest and the oldest were five in a late-twenties, early-thirties age group. All of them were redheads, at least two not naturally so. All had lost the bloom of youth still possessed by the frightened girl but would be easy on the eye for a long time yet. It was impossible to judge their figures, for all the women were attired in identical cream serge nightgowns, buttoned at the throat but otherwise untrimmed and shapeless.

Like the young girl, they had snatched handguns from beneath

9

their blankets the instant they recovered from the shock of the rude awakening. They were uneasy rather than afraid: and had the presence of mind to pull back the hammers of the Colts, and the composure to maintain a steady aim.

'You ain't been in Houston lately, mister,' the old woman growled.

'Never have been there at all, ma'am,' Steele replied. He appeared calm, but inside he was having to censure himself against futile rage. He had keyed himself to counter an unknown danger, then had relaxed his guard before he knew the full facts of the situation in the hollow. He had ignored the lessons of the past.

'Explains why you ain't never heard of Mrs Lucifer and Satan's Daughters.' She spoke the group's title with more than a hint of pride.

'He's lyin', madam!' the frightened eighteen-year-old cried. 'You said you would ... '

'I never said I'd murder for you, girl!' the aged leader of the women cut in, her tone rising towards anger. 'Just you let me handle this my way.'

'Yeah, Sal. It's been a lot of miles since the last man. Let's not waste this one if we don't have to.'

The Virginian suddenly felt lightheaded and out of touch with reality – as if he had drunk too much whiskey on a hot day. He was still able to recall the sensations of being drunk – vividly enough so that he never ran the risk of getting that way again. That memory was very old now and it had stood him in good stead to pay heed to it. And yet he had taken the deliberate decision to discount the hard-learned lesson about women – that they were as human, and therefore likely to be as inhuman, as men. The knowledge that he had made this mistake would normally have triggered self-anger and he could have understood this and dealt with it.

But this encounter had a disconcerting aura of the abnormal. Six good-looking women and one ugly one, all of them named for the ruler of hell. All of them aiming guns at him. One demanding he be killed out of hand while another eyed him with calm, sexual appraisal.

Then, as he looked around at their moonlit faces, he saw that it was not just one of them who surveyed him in this way. Two women nodded in agreement with the remark and all of them except the oldest and the youngest responded to his impassive gaze with open stares close to lust.

'Nancy, this is neither the time nor the place!' Mrs Lucifer snapped. 'Kindly get this man's gun.'

Nancy was only slightly miffed by the old woman's tone. And she shrugged this off as she got to her feet to comply with the order. She wore the same style of all-enveloping, shapeless night-gown as the others. But, whether by accident or design, in getting out from under the blankets and standing up, the coarse fabric stretched taut to her flesh and contoured the generous curves of her body.

Some of the other women saw this and showed their resentment, watching sullenly as Nancy emphasised the sway of her hips in approaching Steele.

'Easy, mister!' Mrs Lucifer warned, suspicious of the Virginian's total lack of response as Nancy drew the Colt Hartford from the boot.

'I reckon she is,' Steele replied evenly, meeting the eyes of the woman close to him and reading the frank want in them.

He no longer felt disembodied – a hidden spirit watching himself in an unfamiliar situation. Now there was just an inner struggle against the dangers of anger as he faced up to something he recognised well – the possibility that he would die.

For there was nothing unreal about a group of whores and their madam. It was merely unusual to run across them camped out in a cold night on the western edge of the Llano Estacado. Neither was it strange that they should be afraid of an unshaven and travel-stained man riding unannounced into their camp.

So, with his mental processes functioning normally again, Steele was quickly able to smother the impulse to anger. He considered he had only two dangerous weaknesses and was aware that one of these – a tendency to view all women as the opposite to the worst of men in all things – had caused him to act so carelessly: making him ignore the memories of recent events.

11

'If you got the money, mister, I got the time,' Nancy answered, almost singing the invitation.

She displayed a whore's professional smile and there was just a moment when Steele could have powered off the gelding. To fasten an assassin's scarf around her throat or press the blade of a knife against her flesh.

But he did not trust the young girl with the uncocked Colt to respect the life of a human shield. The other whores were no longer uneasy, recovered from the shock of waking to see him and now watching him simply as a man. The old madam continued to keep him covered with a rock-steady aim, but there was cool reason in her attitude. To the girl, though, he was not merely a man. In her panicked mind he was a special man, come to the camp for a particular purpose. And it would take only an unresponsive squeeze of the trigger and a thumbing back of the hammer to explode bloody violence in the night.

So the Virginian chose to remain seated in the saddle as Nancy backed off, posing no threat with either her revolver or the confiscated rifle.

'Don't you carry no handgun, mister?' Mrs Lucifer growled. She stood up now, tall and broad and as heavy in the body as her face suggested she would be. So that, on her, the nightgown was shapeless and taut at the same time.

'Mostly I get by with the rifle, ma'am.'

There was an inscribed gold plate screwed to the fire-scorched stock of the Colt Hartford. Nancy had spotted it and was filting the rifle so that she could read in the moonlight the lettering cut into the metal.

'To Benjamin P. Steele, with gratitude, Abraham Lincoln,' she recited.

One of the others gasped, as if impressed by the name of the former president.

'Old Abe's dead, Steele,' Mrs Lucifer growled. 'And even if he wasn't, he wouldn't cut no ice with me, so . . . '

'Ben Steele's dead as well,' the Virginian interrupted. 'He was my Pa. I'm Adam Steele.'

'Hi, Adam,' Nancy greeted. 'This ain't exactly the Garden of Eden, but if you're lookin' for an Eve, I . . . '

'Let it be!' the madam snarled, with a fast glare at Nancy. Then the youngest whore vented a low moan and the old woman switched her angry look to another subject. The power of her feelings dragged the girl's awareness away from Steele. The other women also looked towards the madam and there was tacit mockery in their faces. For stretched seconds of cold silence only the Winchester was aimed with menace at Steele. And even this threat had a quality of emptiness: so that he sensed he could merely wheel his horse and ride away. Except that he did not have the rifle, and the girl's terror was not gone: merely subdued.

'So what do we do now?' Nancy taunted to break the silence. 'Say we're sorry for actin' like scaredy cats, pat him on the head and send him on his way?'

She smirked as she spoke and a darkening glare of deepening anger on the madam's face failed to dislodge it. Then Mrs Lucifer's gaze darted this way and that over every face: to discover that Steele's expression of calm resignation was the least discomfiting to look at.

'What's the idea of creepin' up on us, Steele?' she rasped.

'Was that what I did?' he countered.

He was now as relaxed as he looked. The fat and ugly old madam was the undisputed leader of the group, with enough influence to sway events despite the depth of feelings of the younger and more emotional women.

'I sure didn't know you was comin' until I opened my eyes and saw you.'

'Reckon that just means you ladies are sound sleepers.'

She tossed her head, irritated by his even-voiced responses to her sour-toned questions. 'Why'd you come here?'

'Happened to be between the place I came from and where I'm going to, ma'am,' he answered, stretching the truth just a little.

The young girl snorted her disbelief.

Mrs Lucifer lowered the Winchester until it was aimed at a point between the gelding's forehooves. Except for the girl with the uncocked Colt, all the other women were equally as casual in the way they held their guns.

The madam gave an emphatic nod of her head and took some

of the harshness out of her voice. 'Then we won't hold you up no longer, mister. You best get goin' to wherever it is you're headed.'

'After we said we're real sorry for pullin' guns on you, Adam,' Nancy augmented. And there was genuine sadness in her voice and expression. But not, Steele guessed, for the reason she stated.

Then the fires of anger flared again in the madam. And she licked her lips and formed her mouthline into a hard scowl as Steele shook his head.

'Never go anyplace without my rifle.'

'If you think I'm goin' to give you back your gun . . . '

She curtailed the retort with a gasp. And swung her Winchester up to cover him again. The frightened young girl vented a choked scream and stared down in horror at the Colt in her two-handed grip as it failed to explode when she squeezed the trigger.

The other five women remained no more than amused spectators to the panic: which was caused by Steele swinging easily out of the saddle. He reached the ground with his back to the group, in a half crouch, as he began to unfasten the cinch leathers.

But he swung his head towards a flurry of sounds: and was in time to see Nancy stooping over the young girl. She had dropped her own Colt and was in the process of snatching away the other girl's gun, just before the hammer could be cocked.

'You should have stayed home, little girl!' Nancy growled. 'Pretty soon we'll all be as crazy scared as you are.'

Standing on the tough grass of the hollow, Steele saw he had judged the situation correctly and that the danger was past. The girl had been disarmed and the old woman was afraid. Not of him. Instead, of her own reaction to his unexpected move. He had taken a calculated risk, which was nothing new to him. The tension had been slight and drained quickly out of him.

'You've got a problem, ma'am,' he told Mrs Lucifer. 'Maybe six of them. So you don't need me if you reckon I'm another one. But seems you've got me unless you give me back my rifle.'

'I have no intention of . . . '

'That sounds definite enough,' Steele cut in, turning his back

14

on the women again and restarting the chore of unsaddling the horse. He sensed eyes watching him – uneasy and amused – as he continued: 'So I reckon you're stuck with me until morning. Don't want to be any trouble. I'll sleep under the coach. Breakfast will be fine if you plan it. If not, just coffee.'

He pulled the saddle and bedroll clear of the gelding, slung the gear over his shoulder and turned to show his boyish smile to the women. Five of the whores responded with grins. The girl's fear deepened. Mrs Lucifer's face was suddenly purple with indignation that the initiative had been stolen from her.

'I ought to have blasted you right at the start!' she managed to force out between clenched teeth as the Virginian ambled along the line of women.

He halted in front of her and shook his head, allowing the smile to fade from his bristled features. 'You're no killer, ma'am. And nor are any of the others.'

'Unless we have to be,' Nancy said without emotion.

'Took that into account,' Steele went on, unconcerned by the remark. 'But I didn't stop by to start trouble of any kind. So you ladies haven't made any mistakes that matter. Come the light of day, maybe you'll be able to see that.'

He heard a sharp intake of breath behind him and powered into a turn. There was no time for self-anger now. Just to feel fear as a hard, ice-cold ball at the pit of his stomach. Before he wrenched his eyes away from the fleshy face of Mrs Lucifer, he glimpsed triumph in a new set of her lips and realised she was in command again. That the minor rebellion of the women had been shortlived – perhaps even a pretence to put him off his guard again.

Then he saw Nancy's expression of grim determination. And a sea of other faces patterned from the same emotional mould. Nancy was down on her haunches, swinging her body from the waist. Both her arms were out at full stretch, her hands fisted around the frame of the Colt Hartford.

He controlled the fear and faced the inevitable fact that he was in the wrong attitude to leap clear. All he could do was force himself into a forward fall to lessen the impact of the blow. But it was merely a token defence of a man resigned to defeat. The

15

rifle barrel slammed into the backs of his knees and his legs bent. His body whiplashed first forwards, then backwards and he hit the ground hard: staying on his knees for a part of a second.

The fires of agony exploded from his legs to rage through his body. And the roaring in his ears as he struggled to stifle a vocal response to the pain made the shouts of the women seem to be coming from a great distance. For part of the same second he saw them lunging towards him, their faces and shapelessly clothed bodies blurred by the salt moisture of pain's tears. Then he was knocked on to his side and jerked out full length as hands clawed at him and a great, blanketing weight of female flesh was pressed down on him.

'Don't just stand there, girl!' he heard Mrs Lucifer shriek. 'Get some rope from the coach!'

He struggled, hating the loss of dignity more than he feared for his life. At least three women had flung themselves across him, at his legs, belly and head. Both wrists and one ankle were firmly trapped by long-nailed hands. His kneecaps felt as if they had been shattered and his lungs were filled with stale air trapped by the weight of a woman pressing her midriff against his face. Exhaustion came quickly.

'Get off his head, you stupid bitch!' Nancy snarled. 'You'll friggin' suffocate the poor bastard!'

'Don't you call me a stupid bitch, you stupid bitch!'

But the smothering effect of her body was abruptly ended. She bobbed up and Steele could see the glinting stars on the inky sky. His free ankle was clutched by strong hands. He expelled the old air and gratefully sucked in a fresh supply from the night. His body demanded more of the same and he breathed fast, only vaguely aware of events around him as he fought to recover from the attack. But the pains in his legs began to rage again as soon as he had doused the fires in his chest.

And he was a prisoner by then. His legs were bound at the ankles and his wrists were lashed together. Then somebody sat him up and pushed his arms down in front of him. Two others wound a length of rope around him several times and knotted it, to trap his elbows and forearms to his chest and belly.

They backed away from him and he had to make a conscious

effort to keep from flopping over on to his back. So he sat, his gear on one side of him and his crumpled hat on the other, breathing almost normally now. It was his captors, standing in a half circle in front of him, who were breathless after the exertion of making him a prisoner.

'And I reckoned you liked me,' he accused Nancy, trying for a light tone and failing.

'She likes all men, feller,' a woman at the end of the line answered.

'But there ain't one I'd trust further than I could toss him by his . . .'

'Nancy!' Mrs Lucifer shrieked. 'Watch your language!'

The old woman was merely shocked. But Nancy was verging on anger as she continued to glare at Steele. But she controlled it and her tone held just the faintest timbre of strain.

'I like men, Adam Steele, that's for sure,' she allowed. 'Because I need them. But that don't mean I have to let them walk all over me just on account they're men and I'm a woman.' Her expression calmed and she glanced at Mrs Lucifer. 'I'm all through now, madam.'

The old woman looked around at the others and nodded her satisfaction when she saw they had all become as subdued as Nancy.

'Good!' she announced at length. 'You have all done well, but whether all this was really necessary . . . ' She shook her head. 'We will make this gentleman as comfortable as possible under the circumstances. And come mornin' I will decide what to do about him. Bed him down under the coach and one of you attend to his horse.'

Nancy was among the four who moved forward to lift Steele. 'You carry a lot of weight for such a little feller,' she forced out between clenched teeth.

'I told you I didn't plan on being a burden to you ladies,' the Virginian answered. This time his voice hit the right note of levity.

'You wouldn't have if you'd just rode on by,' somebody growled.

He was conscious of being watched and sensed animosity in a

fixed stare. It was not difficult to trace the source to the elfin-faced young girl. She seemed rooted to the spot, determined not to touch Steele or anything that was his.

'Next time I'll know,' he muttered, recalling for a moment the women of Borderville, New Orleans and Rain.

He was carried to the parked Concord and lowered gently to the ground. Two of them unfurled his bedroll, then covered him with blankets. A third went to help with the hobbling of his gelding. Nancy stood and watched the frightened and hate-filled young girl, silent until she was alone with Steele. Then she crouched down beside him.

'If that crazy little girl ever points a gun at you again, Adam, there's a good chance there won't be a next time for anythin' for you.'

'You want me to say I'm grateful?' he asked.

'No,' she said huskily, reaching under the Concord to raise his head and push his crumpled hat beneath it for a pillow. 'It was as much in my interest as yours to keep you alive.' She began to breathe faster as her hands moved from his head to his shoulders, her fingers crooking into claws. 'And there's only one thing I want from you, you muscular sonofabitch.'

Her exploring hands travelled to his upper arms.

'Nancy Maguire, come on out of there!' Mrs Lucifer roared.

'Damn her!' the aroused woman gasped, tearing her hands away from Steele.

'With a name like hers, I reckon she's already gone to the devil,' the Virginian muttered.

'I'll be back, Adam Steele.'

'Yeah,' he said softly as she rose and turned away. 'Seems a man's got to screw what a man's got to screw.'

Chapter Two

The women did not re-light the fire before they bedded down again and for a long time Steele allowed his imagination free rein. Just the sight of the dead ashes emphasised the bitter cold which penetrated the blankets and his clothing to attack his flesh. And he began to hate the inanimate, burnt out wood: blaming it completely for his suffering.

For he had entered into a kind of waking dream again: this time held on that thin line between sleep and awareness of reality. But, even in imagination, his predicament and the manner by which he had allowed it to come about was ridiculous. And it was recognition of this which triggered a different kind of coldness within him. The familiar icy ball of self-anger which was just a degree removed from fear. And as it swelled from his belly to engulf his entire body, it served to clear his mind of futile incredulity.

The real reason why he felt so cold was the first logical thought to enter his head: it was simply because the tightness of his bonds hampered the circulation of his blood. Then he considered the knife in his boot sheath: but remained unmoving beneath the blankets in the deep moon shadow cast by the Concord. For he sensed watching eyes.

He was lying on his back, his head screwed to the side on his hat so that he could see the entire campsite merely by swinging his eyes in their sockets. Five of the women were sleeping, anxious to comply with Mrs Lucifer's order that they should get all the rest they could before dawn. But the lusting Nancy Maguire and the frightened young girl remained awake, nurturing their powerful emotions as they peered out of the shadows of their blankets towards the unmoving and indistinct form of the Virginian.

When he did move, he thought he heard a low gasp. But then the sounds of the camp reverted to what they had been before – the regular intaking and expelling of breath as women slept, or feigned sleep. He moved to put his back to the watching women, tucking his head down on to his chest and drawing up his knees in what was almost a foetal position. His legs still hurt from the blow and fall and the tightness of the bonds further hampered the move. But he trapped the involuntary cry in his throat. Then remained still, except for an emphasised raising and lowering of his shoulders as he, too, pretended to be asleep.

Had they known him, the two women who stayed awake would have realised something was wrong. For the Virginian appeared to be sleeping deeply and this was something he had not done since the War Between the States – when he had learned that such a luxury could get a man killed.

He had learned many other lessons, too, riding as a cavalry lieutenant for the Confederacy. Living without the luxuries which were his as the son of one of Virginia's richest plantation owners had been relatively easy to assimilate. It had been much more difficult – even painful – to accept that the skills he had acquired for pleasure had to be employed for killing his fellow human beings: until brutal combat on blood-run battlefields had driven home to him the grim truth that he had to kill to stay alive.

So he had used his abilities as a horseman, hunter and rifleman to seek out and destroy as many of the enemy as opportunity afforded him. And, as events forced upon him the necessary change from a rich and privileged sportsman to a killer in uniform, he honed his old skills and developed new ones.

At the opening of the war he had held the Confederate cause in high esteem: to such an extent that he respected his father's decision to support the Unionists. But few men survived the war with the ideals they held at the start: and Adam Steele lost his early, amid the noise and stink and the pain of brutalising battles. And each grey-clad corpse he saw sprawled in the mud or spread-eagled on sun-baked earth made him more embittered, more determined to survive and slaughter. Not for a political cause any more – simply to protect himself from becoming a bullet-riddled or shell-shattered corpse. And it was inevitable that he should grow to hate his father for aiding those who sought to kill him.

The the grim war ended and it was incredible to Steele that he should be influenced by the euphoria of peace. But he was so affected and, like countless thousands of other survivors – whether victorious or defeated – he discovered he was ready and anxious to rejoin the human race and re-adopt its values.

Some, however, were not so willing to leave old scores unsettled. And on the April night when Abraham Lincoln was assassinated, Ben Steele was lynched. In a Washington bar-room where he had been waiting for his son, impatient for a promised reconciliation and a new beginning to the old, rich life.

This act of cold-blooded murder had dictated there could be no peace for Adam Steele until he had tracked down the killers and avenged the death of his father. He did what he had to do, but in such a manner that he was forever doomed to be cut off from the life he had intended to rebuild. For, such was his thirst for vengeance, that he killed recklessly: even wantonly. And, just as had happened in the war, he left the innocent as well as the guilty slumped in ugly death behind him. But the war was over and Steele had neither a uniform nor a justifiable cause to excuse the brutal killing.

Among the dead was a deputy sheriff named Jim Bishop who had been sent from the east into the west to arrest Adam Steele. And in killing this lawman the Virginian had sealed his fate for all time: not simply because he had murdered a deputy and had thus placed himself totally outside the law. Far more important to Steele was the fact that Bish had been his best friend.

So, as he lay on his side, curled up beneath the Concord

coach, the Virginian was able to suffer the pain and the cold and the humiliation of his position better than most men. For he had endured such hardships many times before, in war and during the violent peace which had begun in that Washington bar-room. And he almost always learned from his experiences.

'Except where women and easy money are concerned,' he murmured through pursed lips, acknowledging his two weaknesses as the rope binding his ankles parted.

He had not been accentuating the movement of his shoulders simply in a pretence of sleep for its own sake. The action had enabled him to reach into the split seam on the outside of his right pants leg, draw the knife from the boot sheath and then saw at the rope. All this without alerting the two women who he sensed were still staring into the moon shadow beneath the coach.

The manner in which he carried a knife and the skill with which he could use it as a lethal weapon had their beginnings in the war. It had been a different knife then, but that one had been lost somewhere. Just as the derringer which he had used to fire the first shot in the violent peace had been lost. Also gone was the stickpin with the ornate head which had become a weapon when the occasion demanded. Now he relied on the Colt Hartford rifle – his sole legacy from a once wealthy father – the new knife and the silken scarf with its weighted corners.

How many lives had these weapons taken? In war and peace. How many times had he escaped death because he had learned so well the arts of killing?

As he pretended a movement in sleep, drawing his knees up higher and clamping the handle of the knife between his thighs, he made a mental tally. Counting corpses to combat pain and cold and anger. Reliving the horrors of the past so that there was no opportunity to dwell on the events of the present. Putting into practice another well-learned lesson as he ran the rope at his wrists up and down the length of the sharp blade.

While he was engaged in this, one woman drifted into an uneasy sleep. Another remained achingly awake.

A second length of rope parted and the Virginian eased his legs out straight, bunching and relaxing his muscles against

22

cramp and relishing the minor triumph. He was able to curtail his mental exercise now, in full command of his senses and emotions as he completed the act of freeing himself. For the adrenalin of success was pumping through his body and this was sufficient to swamp the discomforts which had previously threatened to hamper him.

The only danger now was impulsive recklessness, but he had already made one such mistake tonight: when he rode down into the hollow, ignoring his instinct for caution. It was too recent for him to repeat such an error. So he continued to free himself at the same unhurried pace as before, conscious of watching eyes and careful to ensure that no move he made would arouse suspicion.

Then he rested, abruptly a victim to bone-deep exhaustion: from a day in the saddle under the blistering Texas sun and better than two early morning hours of cold, sweating tension as he struggled for release from the humiliation of his capture.

Next he rolled over on his back.

Nancy Maguire gasped and Steele had to fight the threat of anger again: a brand of rage which, like before, was not directed at the woman for surprising him: instead was turned inwards at himself for failing to be aware of her closeness until he saw her.

She recovered from the shock of his sudden move and smiled her relief as she dropped to her haunches.

'Everyone's asleep, Adam,' she whispered. 'Even that crazy little rich bitch. So if you'll stay quiet, you'll have the time of your life.'

The Virginian's mood also eased. For he realised he was still draped from his neck to his boots by the blankets. So the woman who clawed her hands and reached under the coach for his shoulders was unable to see the severed ropes and the knife which he clutched in his right hand. And in the darkness his face was nothing more than a blur: an unidentifiable mask of paleness that concealed the fleeting glare of anger he showed.

'What if I yell rape?' he rasped in response to her husky whisper, and the thin line of his teeth between curled-back lips gleamed very white against his dark bristles.

She withdrew her hands and hiked her nightgown so that the coarse fabric was bunched at her belly. Then responded to his wryly mocking smile with a broad grin as she parted her thighs: to reveal their smooth, white nakedness in submissive invitation all the way into the dark shadow of her luxuriantly bushed sex.

'You're all man, Adam,' she countered, sensuously licking her lips. 'So you won't do nothin' but enjoy what you got comin' to you.'

She stood up then, drawing in a deep breath of excitement, hooked her hands inside the neckline of the nightgown and pushed her arms high above her head. The hem of the unflattering garment travelled fast up the length of her legs, her body and her head. To come clear as she leaned forward, her heavy breasts losing their perfect conical shape to sag long with their weight.

'And I reckon you're all woman,' the Virginian replied, feeling a vague stir of arousal as his dark eyes raked over her white flesh with its patches of shading at the base of the belly, crests of the breasts and under the armpits. Despite his knowledge that she was a whore with the bloom of youth ill-used out of her, he knew that under different circumstances he might have found it easy to allow his feelings to expand.

'Figure to show you just how much of one, Adam,' she rasped, dropping down on to her haunches again and reaching out with both hands to grasp the blankets at his neck.

'Well, look what we found us here, boys!'

'Damnit, not again!' Nancy groaned. She snatched her hands away from the blankets and powered erect in a whirling turn, grasping her nightgown and pressing it against the front of her naked body.

Steele moved only his head at the sound of the strange voice, to peer around the angrily frustrated woman towards the top of the knoll where he had first looked down at the campsite.

Four men were up there, in the process of releasing the reins by which they had led their horses: to draw revolvers and aim them down as the other women were jerked awake and vented their shock.

24

'A whole friggin' herd of 'em, Rufus!' another man yelled gleefully.

'I see 'em, Walt! I see 'em!'

'Damnit, damnit, damnit!' Nancy snarled, struggling to get her nightgown the right way up and pull it back on.

Mrs Lucifer was screaming at the whores, the meaning of what she said lost under the barrage of shouts they hurled at the strangers and at each other.

A man added his cursing voice to the din, as all the rudely awakened women except the youngest scrambled to their feet: and swung their guns towards the hill crest. Imitating the actions of Mrs Lucifer as she abandoned the struggle to make herself heard.

But it was the men who fired first. Even though they had started to holster their guns when they thought they had stumbled upon a camp of defenceless women. Four revolvers bucked. And the screams of the women rose in shrill panic as the bullets cracked through the night air to dig up divots of dry earth among the disturbed bedrolls.

'Shuddup!' Rufus bellowed. 'Stop the friggin' noise!'

Two of the women had pitched themselves to the ground as the gunshots exploded. Another had flung her Colt out in front of where she appeared suddenly to be rooted to the spot. With the always frightened young girl still huddled beneath her blankets and Nancy fighting to get her nightgown back on, this left just Mrs Lucifer and one of the whores with guns trained up at the intruders.

But the crack of gunfire and the harsh command had the effect of staying their fingers on the triggers as the sounds of panic were curtailed.

'And you, woman!' Walt roared in a voice of mixed anger and joy. 'Just ain't no point in you gettin' all dressed up again!'

'Listen to me!' Rufus snarled. 'We could've drilled four of you right then! Sure will drill both of you if you don't drop them guns!'

The younger woman, holding her Colt out at full arm stretch in both hands, looked desperately at Mrs Lucifer. The woman with the Winchester stood as a statue, aiming the rifle like an

25

expert sharpshooter at one of the targets skylined against the night on the hill crest.

'Come to that!' the obvious leader of the bunch augmented, menace thickening his tone, 'we can afford to drill six of you fillies and still screw all we want.'

'Long as it ain't the old biddy we get left with, Rufus,' the man on his right growled. And cackled with laughter.

'Madam?' the woman with the Colt implored.

Mrs Lucifer held her rigid stance for a moment longer. Then her head dropped forward, she swayed and almost stumbled over the hem of her nightgown as she took a sideways step to steady herself. Her arms sagged to her sides as if the strength had suddenly drained out of them. But she continued to grip the Winchester by the frame and barrel across her bulbous belly.

'Get rid of the gun, lady! Or I get rid of you.' As he made the new threat, Rufus swung his revolver to draw a bead on Mrs Lucifer.

The younger woman released her Colt and the soft thud as the gun hit rumpled blankets seemed to snap the older one out of her private world of misery. And there was resignation on her fleshy face as she raised her chin up from her chest and looked around at the whores.

'Men are nothin' new to any of you,' she pointed out, low enough so that the men on the hill could not hear.

She looked towards Nancy Maguire last of all. The woman had complied with the order from the hill top and now simply clutched her nightgown to the front of her body. As Mrs Lucifer saw this, she expressed brief disgust.

'Drop the friggin' rifle, lady!' Rufus insisted.

It was as if Mrs Lucifer had forgotten about them while she stared scornfully at Nancy. But the harsh voice cut through the futile train of thought and, as she started to turn, she glimpsed the indistinct form of Steele in the Concord's moon shadow. And desperate hope shone briefly in her eyes.

Then, with apparent carelessness, she tossed the Winchester towards the front of the coach. A single spark flew as the barrel struck a wheelrim.

'Real fine and dandy!' Rufus called. Abruptly happy again as he started to lead his horse down the slope, his revolver still aimed.

The other three men trailed him, grinning from behind their negligently held guns.

'Move away from the coach, ma'am,' Steele rasped softly. 'Reckon you and the others know how to keep those fellers occupied.'

Nancy snapped her head around to look down at him, her mouth gaping open.

'Guess it's hard for you, but forget you're a woman for a couple of seconds,' he put in before she could make a sound. 'Do something without talking.'

'My father sent them,' the terrified young girl moaned from under her blankets. 'It's a trick. I know it is. He sent them. He wants me . . . '

Steele had eased his hands into sight. And the girl's fear-filled voice acted to free Nancy from the shock of realising that the Virginian was no longer a prisoner.

'Shut your mouth until one of these fellers tells you to open it, Sally! And they sure won't want you to use it for talkin' with!'

Her voice was hard and brittle as she strode away from the Concord. And a bright, paper-thin smile was suddenly pasted to her face. But none of the men saw this. For, as she moved out of the moon shadow cast by the coach she let go of the shielding nightgown: and none of the intruders was able to tear his wide eyes away from the pale nakedness of her swaying body.

All the women except Sally and Mrs Lucifer also stared at her, their shock as compulsive as the mounting lust of the men.

And the words she continued to yell ensured that she remained the centre of attention as she came to a halt beside the dead fire, her legs splayed and her bunched fists resting on the curves of her hips.

'You fellers want to get laid, you came to the right place! This here's Mrs Lucifer and we're Satan's Daughters! We been the best there ever was in Texas and we aim to spread ourselves far and wide across the Territories and California. Maybe you ain't never heard of us if you ain't never been to Houston. But you'll know us real well before this night's over, I'm bettin'.'

As Nancy flaunted her naked body, turning this way and that to provide visible proof of her sexuality, Steele pulled on the buckskin gloves. Then eased forward and pushed a hand out from under the coach to grasp the barrel of the Winchester.

'But we ain't your ordinary run-of-the-mill whores, gents!' Nancy went on, keeping her voice high as the incredulously surprised men ambled closer. 'Satan's Daughters ain't really whores at all! We dance, gents! And we sing! We play all manner of instruments! We're the best entertainers in the business! And after the show, we're available, gents!'

For a while, the Virginian listened to the meaning of what Nancy was saying instead of merely hearing the sound of her shrill voice. And found himself intrigued, unable to believe she had plucked the story from her imagination. But then he vented a low grunt of disgust, chiding himself for failing to concentrate entirely on what he had to do.

Just one pair of eyes watched as he carefully inched the Winchester into the cover of the moon shadow beneath the Concord. Those of Mrs Lucifer as her fleshy face continued to pretend to show shock at Nancy Maguire's words and actions. Steele grunted again, then drew back his lips from his teeth to show a silent snarl. It was unlikely the old woman saw or heard the Virginian's reaction. Probably she simply realised she was endangering the result of the makeshift plan she had triggered into being. And she wrenched her attention away from the coach, to give the younger woman some support.

'All right, Nancy,' she snapped, and showed a welcoming smile to the men as they neared the foot of the slope. 'Pardon me, gentlemen, but you are seeing the end of the performance before the beginning!' She spread her arms out to either side and raised them high. 'Stand up, ladies. So that I can introduce you to the customers. I'm certain they will treat us respectfully when they realise the kind of ladies we are!'

The Virginian certainly did not have to make any effort to keep a grip on reality now: as he bellied backwards over the ground to emerge into moonlight on the side of the Concord

28

away from the advancing quartet of incredulous men. For he was no longer a prisoner of this strange group of women and there was a rifle in his gloved hands. It was a Winchester instead of the familiar Colt Hartford: but it was more than he had any right to expect after allowing himself to be taken so easily.

He stood up slowly, his bristled face wincing into a grimace at the pains in his legs, and turned the handle of the door. The clicks of the mechanism and the creak of the hinges as he pulled open the door were covered by the strident voice of Mrs Lucifer.

'Nancy you already know! This is Gertrude. And Faith. That is Hope. That one Charity. The shy girl is Sally, gentlemen. She's new to our company and I'd ask you to treat her very gently because . . . '

'They're from my father!' Sally shrieked across Mrs Lucifer's introductions. 'I know they are! You said you'd protect me!'

Steele closed the door and froze for a stretched second, peering across the width of the coach and out of the windows on the far side. The four men were down in the hollow now, on level ground and in a position to have seen his humped form had he still been under the vehicle. But he had climbed aboard in time. The only danger was that they had seen the Concord tilt as he entered.

Then he saw that this had never been a risk. For it was the men on the edge of the campsite who were caught between reality and a sense of the unreal now. Cowhands, by the look of them. Dressed in Stetsons and windcheaters, with chaps over their pants and spurs on their boots. Three of them about forty and the fourth in his early twenties. All standing close to six feet. Leading horses laden with well-equipped saddles.

They stood, guns still carelessly held, staring wide-eyed and open-mouthed at the madam and whores.

'Be best if you just ignore her, gentlemen,' Mrs Lucifer urged, her voice not so loud now that the men were close. Then she shook her head as if to physically rid herself of the anxiety which had crept into her lowered tone. 'She's not properly trained yet. But the rest of my ladies, they have been with me for a long time. But I want to repeat what Nancy told you,

29

gentlemen. They are not whores to be bought for a few dollars for a few minutes. They are fine entertainers who are willing to make themselves available after the show.'

'Don't give a shit what they are, you old bag!' Rufus growled. 'So long as they're women who got what women supposed to have. Like the one already stripped off.'

'Hard to see if they all got that,' Walt said huskily. He was the youngest of the quartet.

The other two snapped their lips closed, signalling that they had also emerged from the near trance into which they had been plunged by Nancy's brazen display.

Then all four raked their eyes along the line of standing women as Rufus snarled: 'Strip off! And that means you as well, girl!' He swung his Remington to aim it at the trembling form of Sally contoured by her blankets. 'Me and the boys got a lot of ballin' to catch up on.'

'Sure has been a long trip from Denver,' Walt agreed, excitement continuing to thicken his voice.

'Do as he says, ladies!' Mrs Lucifer said quickly, with a glance towards the Concord. 'It is obvious these gentlemen cannot spare the time for preliminaries.'

'Damn right, you old bag!' Rufus retorted, unable to tear his stare away from the blanket-draped form of Sally. 'Men as hungry as we are don't need no starters.'

Steele had crossed from one side of the coach to the other, his gloved thumb cocking the hammer of the Winchester. He sat now in a corner seat, pressing himself against the backrest so that he would not be silhouetted in the windows. But he could see the entire scene in the hollow.

His gelding and the team horses contentedly cropped at the tough grass on one side of the fire which had been out for so long. On the other side, Mrs Lucifer was closest to him. Beyond her, an abruptly subdued Nancy Maguire, looking pathetic in her nakedness now that she was unable to sustain the pretence of wanton abandon.

Between Nancy and the line of four women beginning to pull off their nightgowns was the completely covered Sally.

Directly opposite the Concord stood the four unshaven and

travel-stained cattle drovers: expressing brutal lust as they released the reins of their horses. Then they stepped forward.

'I told you to get out from under them blankets, girl!' Rufus snarled, ignoring the nakedness of the compliant women as he advanced on Sally's bedroll. And he pasted on to his face a grin that was as vicious as his tone. 'But if you ain't gonna do like you're told, it makes it better for me. Worse for you.'

There had been few good times for Steele since the start of the war that was a prelude to the violent peace. So that, if ever he felt the need to catalogue events since fate forced him to trade one kind of life for another, he would judge them by the degree of evil surrounding them.

Recently there had been a time that was very bad. Perhaps as bad as when he found his father's body hanging from a beam. Or equal on the scale of evil with the death of Jim Bishop and its Mexican aftermath. A time on the Mississippi River when the innocent as well as the guilty had died – for no better cause than greed for money. He might have died in the ghost town of Rain because he was still suffering a reaction to what had happened aboard the northward bound sternwheeler. But it was decreed that he should survive while many others came to violent ends – not one of them at his hand.

Which were the guilty and which the innocent here in this hollow? A bunch of whores who had caused him physical and mental suffering and some women-hungry cowhands looking for a good time. Neither group any of his business: except in the negative aspect that he had good reason not to help the women.

'Man, oh man, oh man!' Walt groaned as he halted in front of Charity and raked his eager eyes over her naked body.

Gertrude vented a choked cry of dismay as a man clutched a hank of her red hair and pulled her close to him, arching his back to press his belly against hers.

A third man rested both hands on the shoulders of Faith and bore down, forcing her to kneel in front of him.

The untouched Hope stood like a moonlit statue, gazing in horror as the trio of men groaned their ecstasy at the first contact of their rough hands on the soft flesh of the women.

Mrs Lucifer and Nancy Maguire wrenched their eyes away

from the scene and snapped their heads around to stare at the silent Concord.

Rufus stooped, caught hold of a corner of Sally's covering, and snatched it off her.

'You bitch!' he roared, and started to swing his revolver at her.

'I'm not going back!' the girl shrieked. And squeezed the trigger of her Colt.

She held it in a double-handed grip, the heels of her hands and the rear of the butt pressed against her belly. She had remembered to thumb back the hammer this time. And the bullet which exploded from the muzzle went into the open mouth of Rufus before he had time to straighten up. The range was no more than three feet, giving the bullet enough power to pass completely through his head and shatter his skull to gain exit at the crown.

Sally's scream was shrill with pain as the recoil of the big Colt kicked against her belly. But it was horror that became instantly inscribed on her face as blood gushed over her from the gaping mouth of Rufus before he whiplashed erect and then started to crumple.

'Steele!' Mrs Lucifer roared.

Perhaps the Virginian would have taken a hand in this new outbreak of evil without the prompting of the fat old woman. But it was an academic point. She had shouted his name and both she and Nancy were staring at the Concord. Instantly drawing the attention of everyone from the falling corpse of Rufus to the coach. And three revolvers were drawn and swung in the wake of three pairs of horror-widened eyes.

Which put Steele's life on the line.

He threw himself off the seat to the floor, rapping the door handle with the barrel of the Winchester and stabbing the muzzle at the panel.

The door swung wide and he squeezed the trigger. Faith screamed as the man she knelt in front of suddenly fell away from her: rigid as a cut tree, with red sap oozing from a hole in his chest.

Charity was in a half-turn, taking the first stride of a panicked

32

run, as the Winchester exploded a second shot: in perfect time with the thud of the door again the side of the coach. The young cowhand who had been reaching for her breasts ducked instinctively in response to the rifle's muzzle flash. And took the bullet in the centre of his forehead instead of his heart. He rocked backwards: then, with the final shred of his life's strength, fought to straighten. He held upright for part of a second. Finally he corkscrewed to the fire ashes as his legs buckled.

With the same smooth speed as before, Steele pumped the action of the Winchester as he swung the barrel a fraction of a a degree to the left. Then squeezed the trigger again just before the closing door struck the barrel.

As always, he felt nothing which could be termed an emotion as the recoil kicked the stock of the rifle against his shoulder. It was kill or be killed and the kind of life he had was all that was available to him. Perhaps later he would suffer guilt, remorse, mild sorrow or some other brand of mental torment that he had taken life. But in this instant, as he heard a revolver shot echo the more powerful crack of the Winchester, it did not matter.

The whore named Gertrude perhaps saved his life. That did not matter either. All that was important to Steele was that the bullet from the sixgun smashed into the side of the Concord's boot instead of burrowing into his flesh.

The cowhand's aim was spoiled by the whore as she chopped the side of her hand against the nape of his neck. And the blow bent him forward which meant he died a fraction of a second before he otherwise might: pitching on to his belly instead of being sprawled on to his back by the impact of the bullet drilling into his chest.

Gunsmoke drifted in the moonlit air, its acrid taint pungent in the cold of the Texas night. For long moments the only sounds were made by the horses: hoofbeats as the mounts of the cowhands bolted away from the scene of slaughter, and snorts of panic from the hobbled animals.

Nothing else moved.

Until the coach rocked slightly and its springs creaked as Steele got to his feet, pushed open the door and stepped tentatively to the ground. He moved with caution because he was again aware of more mundane things than the fundamental need to stay alive. And his pain-weakened legs felt on the verge of surrendering to the weight they were supporting. His expression was totally impassive: offering no clue to his physical discomfort nor to the depth he was delving into his mind to discover some response to the knowledge that he was responsible for three of the bullet-shattered corpses sprawled on the ground in front of him.

His coal black eyes raked fast over the women, not differentiating between the five who were naked and the two still clad in the shapeless nightgowns. The women responded to his bleak and cursory survey with either rigid horror or trembling fear. And did not utter a sound as the Virginian moved to Nancy's dishevelled bedroll, where he stooped to trade the Winchester for the Colt Hartford.

Then he looked at the dead men and the living women again: and vented a grunt of satisfaction that his conscience remained clear. This small sound stirred Mrs Lucifer to a vocal response.

'Thank you, Mr Steele,' she croaked, then cleared her throat noisily. 'I hate to think what would have happened to us had you not been here to help us.'

The Virginian pursed his lips, then curled them back from his teeth to show a cold grin. The expression felt at home there, despite the sights and stinks of violent death scattered around him – as it always had during the best of the bad times. 'I reckon it was my pleasure, ma'am,' he drawled. 'Even if the ladies didn't have a ball.'

Chapter Three

The first shaft of sunlight which lanced down over the crest of the eastern hillock roused Steele from sleep. And, as always, he came awake to instant awareness and total recall. So he knew why his legs ached and that it was the woman who was speaking who had landed the painful blow.

'. . . and I've said I'm sorry, madam!' Nancy Maguire growled irritably. 'But you know the way I am. And I haven't been with a man since . . . '

'Very well,' Mrs Lucifer interrupted. 'We'll say no more about it. In the event it was very fortunate that you released him and that I had the presence of mind to throw the rifle near the . . . '

Nancy countered the older woman's interruption with one of her own. 'I didn't cut him free, madam.'

The Virginian had bedded down again beneath the Concord: this time with his Stetson over his face and his right hand resting on the Colt Hartford. He rolled out into the bright glare of the warm sun now, placing the hat on his head and canting the rifle to his left shoulder.

'It's not only whores who can do tricks,' he said evenly as all eyes swung towards him.

The women had been busy during what was left of the night after Steele crawled back under the coach. He had heard the activity at first, as they began to obey the orders Mrs Lucifer snapped at them. Then had allowed himself to drift into shallow sleep, still untroubled by his dormant conscience.

And his mind was free of doubts now as he looked at the results of their efforts: the campsite around the blazing fire cleared of all signs of last night's violence. Except for the quartet of geldings now hobbled with the other animals, and a neatly stacked pile of saddles and bedrolls. The corpses had been dragged out of the hollow and the stains of their spilled blood had been covered with dust.

The women had not slept after their chores were completed. They sat now, clad identically in workaday denim dresses of unflattering grey, on folded bedrolls around the rekindled fire. Weary eyed and pale. Holding mugs of aromatic coffee and looking at him with a variety of expressions. Fear and gratitude, shame and concern, dismay and expectancy. Merely a bunch of women in distress. Only Mrs Lucifer had made an effort to improve her appearance – taking the curlers from her blonde hair, brushing it and using paint and powder to gloss over the age wrinkles on her fleshy face. The five redheads and the elfin-like Sally were dishevelled and dirty from panic and work and there was nothing in their commonplace appearance to suggest they were whores.

The cruel brightness of the morning sun shafting down from a cloudless sky served to emphasise their unattractiveness.

'There is somethin' you should know about us, Mr Steele,' Mrs Lucifer said hurriedly as the Virginian stooped, reached under the coach and came erect again with a tin mug in his free hand. 'My ladies are not common whores. So what you did last night . . . '

'I shot three fellers before they could shoot me, ma'am,' Steele told her as he crossed to the fire and went down on to his haunches between Faith and Charity. 'And I got the message you and Miss Maguire were yelling.'

He rested the Colt Hartford across his thighs and reached for the blackened pot among the glowing wood embers.

Mrs Lucifer was insistent that she be heard, but waited until Steele had poured himself a mug of coffee before she went on. 'Satan's Daughters are a group of professional entertainers. The

36

finest anywhere if I do say so myself. Since I gathered them together and trained them. But they are also ladies well versed in the ways of the world. So I have been able to ensure we play to full houses even in those parts of the country where men do not even know the meanin' of the word "culture".'

Steele listened patiently and without a sound or sign of response. He focused his attention on a skillet of water coming to the boil beside the coffee pot and absently rasped the back of a gloved hand over his bristled jaw as he sipped the scalding drink. And his attitude of calm resignation encouraged all but one of the women to accept his presence with the same degree of easiness. Sally was still afraid. But not of him.

'At the end of each performance I draw six ticket stubs from a drum, Mr Steele,' Mrs Lucifer continued.

'Five,' Nancy Maguire corrected, and drew a scowl of anger from the madam. But she refused to be swayed. 'We either trust him or we don't. What's the use of lyin'?'

Mrs Lucifer checked her anger and shrugged her heavy shoulders as she glanced at Sally, who was engaged in a ceaseless survey of the hilltops surrounding the hollow. 'You're right, my dear. I apologise, Mr Steele. Sally Swenson is not one of our company. She is merely sharin' our coach on the trip to Tucson. But there was no point in me tryin' to explain that to those barbarians last night.'

She paused for a comment, but Steele continued to remain silent.

'Anyway, to return to the point that matters now.' She cleared her throat. 'For no charge other than the entrance fee already paid, the holders of the drawn tickets receive the favours of my ladies.' Another pause, then another shrug of the broad shoulders when the Virginian failed to offer a response. 'Two things, sir. Even if my ladies were common whores, the threat they faced last night would have been a very real one. And I thank you for what you did to prevent the incident goin' any further. But my ladies cannot be said to sell themselves. So I'll also thank you not to call them whores.'

Steele nodded now, as Mrs Lucifer compressed her thick lips to signal that she had finished. 'Won't be any trouble, ma'am,' he told her evenly, and was acknowledged by all the group except Sally Swenson as he swung his easy gaze across their weary faces. 'On account that after I've washed up and shaved, I reckon to saddle my horse and leave. Probably I won't ever see you again.'

'That'll be your loss, feller,' Nancy Maguire warned.

'You've got nothing I want, lady,' he replied.

'Time will tell,' the man-hungry woman replied softly, adding seductive lines to her smile.

'I've told you!' Mrs Lucifer snapped.

'And I'm learnin', madam,' Nancy answered.

'That I'm a man who doesn't like to be tied down by women?' the Virginian suggested wryly.

Mrs Lucifer gestured with both hands, as if seeking to brush aside talk that led nowhere. 'What about money, Mr Steele?'

'No, ma'am. Not even if she paid me.'

She was puzzled for long moments, until she saw his boyish grin as he lowered his empty mug from his lips. Then made another gesture with her hands, her painted face grim. 'To accompany us to Tucson, sir. One thousand dollars, payable on arrival.'

Steele sensed one pair of eyes staring at him with greater intensity than the others. And was intrigued to discover the depth of pleading directed at him by Sally Swenson. 'Please agree, Mr Steele,' she implored, then bent her head as she twisted the fingers of her hands together in her lap.

'A lesser amount if you should decide to leave us before we reach our destination,' Mrs Lucifer augmented.

Women and money. Especially easy money. But not easy women. He was no longer grinning as he tried to talk himself out of inviting further trouble. 'You made it from Houston to here without trouble?'

'Yes, we did. But . . . '

'There's no reason why you shouldn't make it all the way to Tucson. Maybe you had your full share of problems last night.'

'And maybe we didn't, Mr Steele,' Gertrude countered.

'I know we didn't!' Sally added forcefully.

'I'll think about it,' the Virginian muttered, stood up fast, canted the rifle to his left shoulder and whirled to head back to the coach. Although his face was impassive, he heard the harshness of his tone, betraying what he felt. And sensed a return to easiness in the minds of the women behind him. Easy women who did not interest him. But offering money, which did.

He did not come erect from under the coach, an open straight razor and a cake of soap in a gloved hand, until he was certain he was in full control of his feelings. And by that time the women had got up from around the fire and were busying themselves with preparations to leave. They worked efficiently and with confidence in their faces, exchanging brief conversations among themselves and ignoring Steele: sure of him.

But, as he stripped to the waist to wash the sweat and dust of travel off his flesh and then scraped at the thick bristles on his face, his imagination played tricks on his conscious mind. He sensed the women casting surreptitious glances towards him as they traded knowing looks and whispered about him. And he felt himself on the defensive again: resenting the women, himself and the position into which he had been manoeuvred.

He took his time, and did not hurry when he saw that the women were ready to leave. Mrs Lucifer was up on the driver's seat, the others were inside the coach and the four saddled geldings of the dead men were hitched on at the back. With slow deliberation, he brushed his teeth, dusted off his clothes and saddled his horse.

They waited patiently for him to finish. Then, when he was astride the mount, gloved hands draped over the saddlehorn, dark eyes gazing out from the shadow of his hat brim in impassive contemplation of physical reality and mental images, Mrs Lucifer said:

'Ready when you are, Mr Steele.'

He nodded, wheeled his horse and rode out ahead of the Concord as the ugly old woman flicked the reins to start the team moving.

It was still early morning and the sun at his back was as yet pleasantly warm. But he knew that with each inch it moved up the eastern dome of the sky its heat would build. He would sweat and the salt moisture would sting his eyes and paste his clothing to his body. Bristles would sprout and itch. Dust from beneath the hooves of the gelding would rise and become ingrained into the countless lines which scored the bronzed skin of his face. He would get thirsty and hungry.

All this was routine to him and he had learned to accept such discomforts and deprivations of the trail because they were an inevitable part of his life. But always he endeavoured to maintain certain standards: was called a dude wherever he went because of his penchant for elegant new clothes and personal cleanliness – consciously indulging himself in minor luxuries as a means of clinging to the last vestiges of the privileged life he once had led. With the subconscious hope that he would one day be able to extend his fingerhold on the past and claw his way back to something akin of what used to be.

But, at the same time, acknowledging that he was not in control of his own destiny: that he was a victim of a cruel fate which decreed he must exist on that knife-edge line between a life of torment and a death of obscene violence.

Such a fate he could understand – regarding it as an instrument of punishment for the crimes he had committed while he tracked down the killers of his father. A substitute for the retribution of man-made law. But why had he allowed himself to become responsible for the safety of this group of whores, their madam and a frightened runaway girl? It was certainly not because they were women in need of help. And the reason had to be better than a mere thousand dollars.

'You mind some company, Adam?'

Again he was startled by the nearness of Nancy Maguire. And angry at himself for being taken by surprise. But things were improving for, as he turned his head to look at her – riding one of the cowhands' geldings alongside – he was able to conceal his feelings behind a mask of impassiveness.

'It's a free country is what they say,' he allowed indifferently.

Either before she boarded the Concord or while it was rolling, she had painted her lips, coloured her eyelids and rouged and powdered her cheeks. She was sweating a little from the exertion of unhitching the horse from the moving coach, swinging into the saddle and riding forward to catch up with him.

But the broad-brimmed hat set on her recently brushed red hair threw a cool shade down over her face and the sweat was no more than an attractive sheen on her skin.

'Country might be free, but no one in it is,' she replied with just a faint trace of bitterness in her tone. 'We're all forced to survive the best way we can.'

'You don't have to make excuses to me, lady,' Steele told her.

'Or *for* you, neither, mister,' she countered.

He did not look directly at her. Simply saw her as one feature of his surroundings as he began to survey the terrain on all sides. He did this involuntarily for the first time since he had led the Concord out of the hollow to begin the westward journey through the range of low hills. And this was another good sign that he was reverting to normal.

His attitude was casual, but Nancy was close enough to see the intensity in his coal black eyes which missed nothing as they raked their bleak gaze over rock and earth, grass and cactus, high ground and hollows.

'You kill real well.'

'When I have to.'

He continued to watch and to wait, listening with a small part of his awareness to the woman riding beside him while the larger share of his concentration was devoted to the hundred and one points of possible threat on all sides.

'And I'm the best lay of our whole bunch. But I'm not advertisin', Adam. Just tellin' you. I'm good because I enjoy what I do. I enjoy men because I need them. And workin' for Mrs Lucifer lets me have what I want and still keep a little self-respect.'

'You telling me anything else?'

'Maybe somethin' that you already know. If you do, you got no right to make moral judgements about us.'

'Did I do that?'

'Not with words. But you done a lot of lookin' at us like we was a bad smell under your nose.'

'Sometimes I've got a nose for trouble, lady. Other times I can see it. Like now.'

His head was swinging slowly from side to side, watchful eyes unblinking and his expression non-committal.

'What?' she asked sharply, and made her own survey. There was fear in her eyes and a hint of panic in the way she wrenched her head around. She saw nothing frightening, but swallowed hard and darted out her tongue to lick beads of sweat from her top lip.

'Indians,' he told her, taking one hand off the reins to point at the ground ahead of the two slow moving geldings.

They were following the course of an arroyo – perhaps the same one the Virginian had paralleled into the hills. In the dust, among the scattering of small rocks and the dried up remains of tree debris, were the imprints of unshod hooves.

Nancy saw the sign and caught her breath. 'How long since they were here? Which way were they goin'? Can you tell that?'

'About six of them going the same way we are,' he answered. 'Droppings a quarter mile back were maybe two hours out of the pony.'

She leaned to the side and turned around, trying to look back beyond the Concord to spot the horse droppings. Abruptly her mind fastened on an idea which subdued her fear.

'Wild horses, maybe?'

'Wild men more like,' the Virginian drawled. 'Drinking whiskey and tossing the empty bottles away.'

Tension made her rigid again. 'You saw one?'

'Two.'

Once more she swallowed hard, but left the sweat beaded on her upper lip. 'Don't you think we should tell Mrs Lucifer, Adam?'

'That isn't her real name, is it?' he countered conversationally.

'Of course not. Her name is Amelia Preston. I said shouldn't we tell her . . . '

'She has problems enough. Why bother her with something she may never have to worry about?'

Nancy was about to pursue the point. Then looked hard at his profile and was calmed by the easy style of his constant vigilance.

'You're very sure of yourself now, aren't you?'

'When I'm working. And right now I've got a thousand-dollar job.'

She stared ahead at the continuing sign in the dust, her blue eyes flicking to left and right for something more substantial than the prints of unshod hooves. Steele peered far beyond what he already knew to be there. His mind was now free of futile considerations about why he had allowed his destiny to become enmeshed with that of the women. For he could engage himself fully with the more concrete problems of a group of drunken Indians and the trouble they could cause.

For almost an hour he rode alongside the woman in silence, as the sun climbed higher and its heat became harsher. Then they were through the range of low hills and heading out across a broad expanse of scrub desert. The Indian sign swung north at the edge of the plain and, for as far as the eye could see into the heat shimmer veiling the western horizon, it was as if nothing had ever moved on the ground until the two geldings stirred the gritty dust.

'Wow,' Nancy sighed. 'I sure wish you'd never mentioned them damn Indians, Adam.'

She relaxed, but Steele remained taut behind his casual veneer. 'They're men. Like any others. Reason I told you about them.'

She shook her head. 'That ain't so. I've heard stories about them. And I've read newspapers. Indians can be real rough with white women.'

Steele licked his lips and spat the dusty saliva to the side. It was an unconscious gesture and it wasn't until after the globule of spit was soaking into the ground that he thought about the act in front of a woman. And, despite the kind of woman she was, he discovered he felt mildly embarrassed. Yet another good sign.

'Rougher than those cowhands back there?'

She clucked her tongue against the roof of her mouth and sighed. 'That was a foul up, mister. It should never have turned out the way it did. Wouldn't have if we never had that crazy Sally Swenson with us. She's had us spooked up ever since she joined us.'

43

'Plain crazy, or crazy scared?' Steele asked, scanning the terrain on all sides but paying particular attention to the area spread away to the north east.

'She's got reason to be scared, the way she tells it. She plans to marry a feller that's waitin' for her in Tucson. But her Pa has other ideas for her. Wants her to marry a man in the cattle business. And he's real sore she ran off, on account of he was fixin' to collect some prime riverside acreage along with a son-in-law.'

'Like you said, lady, nobody's free,' the Virginian drawled.

'Mrs Lucifer was free to tell her to get lost,' Nancy retorted with a burst of anger. 'But she's always been a sucker for a hard luck story. And little miss rich bitch was sure in a spot with a lame horse in the middle of Texas nowhere.'

'That the reason she gave me this job? Because she felt sorry for me?'

The anger was gone and Nancy showed a hard grin. 'She only helps women, Adam. And not because she's strange. She don't like men, that's all. She hired you because she figures she needs you. On account of, like I told you, Sally Swenson has got us all spooked. If we weren't all rattled by her we wouldn't have acted like a bunch of scared Sunday school teachers when you showed up last night. And the cowhands wouldn't be dead.'

'Just dead tired, maybe?'

'Why the hell not?' she snarled, then saw that his mouthline was formed into the boyish grin. And she shrugged off the new impulse to anger. 'I told you, I enjoy my work. All of us do. So we got nothin' to fear from men who just want to have a good time.'

A cloud of dark dust appeared as a contrasting smear on the shimmering heat haze which curtained the north east horizon.

'Except if they're Indians,' Steele reminded, paying scant attention to the dust cloud as he checked for potential trouble in other directions.

'Okay,' she growled. 'And some white men, I guess. But we'd always put out the welcome mat first. And, if they started to get rough, then we'd give them somethin' they didn't plan on. You

44

don't last long in this business without learnin' how to take care of yourself, mister.'

'You want to try that way now? So I can ride on ahead?'

'What?'

He looked hard into the north east and Nancy followed the direction of his gaze. But the dusty cloud had faded and the heat haze was an unmarred line between empty land and sky. Mrs Lucifer saw the concentrated looks on the two faces half turned towards her and snapped her head around to search out the cause.

'What's the matter?' she demanded nervously when she failed to see anything.

'Indians!' Nancy blurted. 'It must be Indians!'

Questions were yelled from inside the Concord as the women struggled with each other to claim the vantage points of the open windows.

'Did you see them?' Nancy asked shrilly, staring into the Virginian's unresponsive profile.

'I reckon.'

'Comin' after us?' Gertrude called.

'Have to wait and see,' Steele answered, reining his horse to a halt.

'Wait nothin'!' Mrs Lucifer snapped and reached for the whip. 'We're goin' to get the hell out of here!'

Nancy hurriedly stopped her mount and backed the animal to stay close to the Virginian. So that the fat woman on the Concord seat was forced to yank on the brake lever and lean back hard to haul on the reins, bringing the vehicle to a skidding halt. The mixture of anger and fear in the glare she directed towards Steele added new lines of ugliness to her face.

'For a thousand dollars, mister, you better do more than just wait and see.'

'Plan to, ma'am. If it's necessary.'

'What?'

'Surprise them.'

'How?' Fear was becoming the dominant emotion as she constantly shifted her eyes from Steele to the distant horizon and back.

45

He swung down from the saddle. 'Seems to me, ma'am,' he replied evenly as he drew the Colt Hartford from the boot and moved in on the Concord with the whores peering out, 'that I've got a whole wagonload of tricks.'

Chapter Four

The dust cloud showed again, dark matt against the wet looking sheen of the shimmering heat veiling the north eastern horizon. And stayed in sight, enlarging as the single scout whose pony had first kicked up the dust was joined by the rest of the braves.

Steele watched the growing blur through a cracked-open blind at one of the Concord's windows and took a firmer grip on the Colt Hartford. Hope, who sat directly opposite him, saw the tightening of the gloved hands on the rifle and caught her breath. Gertrude, Charity, Faith and Sally stared at her tensely and she whispered:

'I think they're comin'.'

'They're coming,' the Virginian confirmed without turning from the window. 'Just remember what I told you.'

'And me,' Sally Swenson added. 'Killing a man who means you harm is easy.'

Steele grimaced at the sentiment expressed by the pretty young runaway. For the first time since he disturbed the night camp, she was not afraid. And that was a cause for concern: for a mind not conscious of reasonable fear was likely to trigger reckless action. In the same way that too much fear could expand to panic with the same result.

But he thought he could rely on the whores and their madam. Certainly they had quietened quickly and listened calmly as he outlined his plan to them: concentrating on what he said even though they cast constant nervous glances towards the empty horizon. He had not told them his belief about fear, for the theory alone was useless. A man – or woman – had to learn from harrowing experience that fear could be a weapon. For if it was controlled it was a guard against rash action and served to hone the reflexes.

As the heavy Concord rolled slowly across the uneven floor of the scrub desert beneath the cruel glare of the blistering sun, Steele spoke softly in the oven heat of the darkened interior.

'Remember, we're doing the unexpected. And the Indians have been drinking whiskey. The scout they sent ahead saw the coach with a driver and two riders in front. Now the whole bunch will see the same thing, except that Nancy's on top with Mrs Lucifer and there are no front riders.'

The five sweating women in the half-light of the Concord listened intently, grim-faced and hands fisted tightly around the cocked Winchesters of Mrs Lucifer and the dead cowhands. Up on the box seat, Nancy Maguire and Mrs Lucifer heard the sound of his drawling voice as just another noise mixed with the clop of hooves, squeak of axles and creak of timber. They were up there because the Virginian considered them to be the most level-headed. And, for the present, they continued to do just as he had instructed: both of them staring directly ahead as Mrs Lucifer held the team to a slow and laborious walk. In a taut, sweating pretence that they were unaware of the advance of the Indians.

'Maybe they picked the scout because he's not a drinker,' Steele continued in the same even tone as the braves cantered clear of the haze so that just the rising dust made them indistinct. 'Or maybe he's as drunk as the rest of them. Whichever, he was looking at us over the same distance we saw him. So he could reckon he made a mistake.'

'They close enough to count yet?' Faith muttered, and raised a hand to brush a strand of red hair from her right eye. She quickly refastened her grip to the Winchester in her lap.

'Five,' the Virginian supplied, and raised his voice. 'Keep facing front, ladies!'

'We're doin' it!' Nancy Maguire growled tensely. 'But you

48

better be as good with that rifle as you claim, mister.'

'He has already proved his skill in that direction,' Mrs Lucifer reminded grimly.

'And I've killed before,' Sally Swenson was quick to point out.

Steele spoke louder now, so that the two women outside the coach could hear him plainly. 'Five of them. Apaches, I reckon. There are no *rancherias* this far east, so they have to be renegades. Mean looking bunch, the way Apaches always are. But don't let that get to you, ladies. They'll be less of a problem than Rufus and his buddies were. No more talk now.'

The five Apaches had eased their ponies down to a trot as they closed to within a half mile of the lumbering Concord: a pace that still enabled them to narrow the gap with every yard that was covered. The dust from beneath unshod hooves did not rise so high now and the Virginian was able to see the braves as separate entities. Young men with unpainted faces flanked by lank black hair trapped at the brow with leather headbands. Naked from the waist up and wearing just leggings and moccasins.

Modern braves running wild and under the influence of the white man in more ways than one. For they had forsaken the bow and arrow pouch in favour of rifle and sixgun. And were drawn towards the enclosed coach by liquor-inspired curiosity: sucked from the same bottle that dulled their inbred hunter instincts.

As they rode to within four hundred yards of the Concord, Steele saw the emaciated thinness of their faces and the sores and scabs of disease on their bodies. Dirt was deeply ingrained into the pores of their flesh. He knew that the fetid atmosphere trapped inside the coach – cloyingly sweet with perfume – would be a pleasant fragrance compared with the stink that accompanied the sweating Apaches.

At a distance of two hundred yards the braves let go of the rope reins and took two handed grips on their rifles. Spencer repeaters which looked as ill-used as the Indians themselves. But just as capable of delivering brutal pain and violent death.

One Apache had emerged as the leader, riding at the centre

and slightly ahead as they used their heels to control the ponies: forming a line abreast to close in on the nearside rear corner of the moving Concord.

As the only one aboard to see them, the Virginian had to consciously practise his theory about fear. For he discovered he was tautly aware of his responsibility for the safety of the women: at last ready to acknowledge his debt to them. A very strange debt, with only Nancy Maguire having an inkling of why it should exist.

Steele was cracking open the blind with the muzzle of the Colt Hartford. Having to struggle against the unreasonable fear that the rifle would slip from his grip – with the grease of sweat that was oozing from the pores of his palms and fingers.

But the buckskin gloves provided a familiar barrier.

He remembered to cluck his tongue against the roof of his mouth.

The women inside the coach heard the small noise above the other sounds, which had now been swelled by the muted clop of unshod hooves against the desert floor. Then he slid off the seat to crouch on the floor.

Hope remained where she was. Sally Swenson moved along the seat to take the place vacated by Steele. Gertrude, Charity and Faith aligned themselves behind the Virginian, imitating his crouching attitude and the way he gripped his rifle – at the frame and barrel with the muzzle aimed at the roof.

Fear seemed to have a palpable presence within the Concord: an invisible heaviness that applied pressure to the flesh of the occupants, squeezing sweat beads from their pores.

There was an abrupt end to the sound of rasping breathing.

A gunshot.

'Oh, my God! Indians!'

'All right! All right!'

Steele let out his breath silently through pursed lips. He saw Hope cross herself. Then the fixed smile of excitement on Sally's face. As the Concord came to an abrupt halt. With Nancy Maguire and Mrs Lucifer still alive to croak the warning and acknowledge it.

A stretched second of silence then, for the Apaches had signalled their ponies to stop.

'You women! No man to drive?'

The brave had to shout. Steele had beaten the dangerous aspect of fear and his entire awareness was working with smooth logic now. So far the incident had gone the way he had predicted. The Apaches, with innate caution but liquored-up foolhardiness, might have approached the enclosed coach in one of two ways. At a flat-out gallop with blazing rifles to put the driver to flight. Or with wary curiosity, as the Virginian had guessed they would if Mrs Lucifer followed his instructions and pretended not to see them until they announced their presence.

'Please, leave us alone!' the ugly old madam pleaded. 'There's just me and my daughter. We have no men.'

'You got whiskey?'

There was no sound of movement, of an advance or a dismount.

'No! We have nothin'! Nothin' you want!'

'You got food? Water?'

The Apache speaking the gutteral English had to shout louder, to be heard above a rumble of words in his native tongue. Then he snarled an order which silenced the braves.

'We know you got food. Water!'

'Yes! Yes, we can spare some!'

Steele felt nothing now. Mrs Lucifer was in tight control of herself and playing her part well. And if Nancy Maguire needed encouragement he knew she would draw it from the older woman. While the four whores and the runaway rich girl inside the coach were as outwardly calm as he was. What happened next was in the lap of the Gods and the responses of the individuals involved. And he trusted only himself.

That was the debt he owed Mrs Lucifer and Satan's Daughters. The regained ability, which he thought he had lost after the slaughter on the *Queen of the River* trip, to act first on the assumption of danger and consider the consequences afterwards. It was not an admirable way to live, but it was the only way for Adam Steele. That had been proved in Rain, but others had acted on his behalf. And it was confirmed when the cowhand named Rufus had taken Sally Swenson's bullet in the head. For the Virginian might easily have been killed by the same gun earlier. But the women had allowed him to live and, except for a few moments of doubt about guilt and innocence, he had acted instinctively in gunning down the other three intruders at the night camp.

And he was ready to kill the Apaches without a moment's hesitation.

'Not some, White Eyes woman! We want all! What else in wagon?'

'Just furniture,' Nancy responded, and it was impossible to tell whether the shrillness in her tone was natural or forced. 'For our new home in California.'

One of the women inside the coach gasped as Nancy spoke the name of the state. It was a signal that the Apaches were advancing, still astride their ponies.

'You get down! Open doors so we see!'

'We have some wine,' Nancy blurted.

This was another code message, to convey the fact that the braves were splitting up, to flank the Concord. There was no movement behind Steele until he wrenched his head around to glower at the women crouched on the floor. Gertrude, who was closest, swallowed hard and turned. Charity and Faith eased on to the seats and slid along them. Gertrude advanced along the floor. There was just a faint rustle of their dress fabric as they took up their positions on the other side of the coach, matching those of Steele, Hope and Sally.

'You got guns?' The voice came from much closer, on the side of the coach where Steele was crouched by the door. At a walk, the unshod hooves of the ponies made hardly any sound at all against the desert floor.

'Just these,' Mrs Lucifer responded. She and Nancy would have lifted two Colts from the seat between them. Holding the weapons by the barrels in a gesture of surrender. The Apaches would be watching the women with the guns. Perhaps all of them. Or just some of them, while the rest peered warily at the Concord with its blinded windows. There was no way anybody inside the coach could know. And Steele had not tried to project the actions of the braves beyond the point at which they closed in on the whites. Nor had he attempted to unburden himself of responsibility by asking Nancy or Mrs Lucifer to signal the time to attack.

He was his own man again. Doing a job in his own way. No longer reluctant to accept the consequences.

'Now,' he rasped softly.

Sally Swenson and Charity worked the door handles. Then all four women on the seats released the blinds at their windows. The slap of the fabric rolled tight by spring pressure was a sound in isolation for a split second.

Then a bedlam of noise broke out.

Cries of alarm from the gaping mouths of the surprised Apaches. Screams of terror from wide-eyed women seeing hostile Indians at close quarters for the first time. The shattering of glass as rifle barrels smashed windows. The crash of flying doors impacting with the sides of the coach.

The crack of rifle fire.

Steele squeezed the trigger of the Colt Hartford as he lunged from the open doorway. And saw the shock inscribed on a brave's face change instantly to agony as the expended bullet drove into his belly. He cocked the hammer while he was in mid-air and had raked the barrel to locate a new target before his boots slammed to the ground. His aching knees protested on impact as he bent his legs to fire from a deep, half-turned crouch. And his lips curled back from his teeth to display a snarling grin of satisfaction. Not that a second brave collapsed to the ground with bright crimson spurting from the side of his head. Instead, that the new victim was already falling: tumbling from a pony that was crumpling under the impact of a bullet in the neck.

For at least one of the women had followed his instructions – to aim at the larger targets of the ponies rather than the riders.

The mount of the first Apache to fall was bolting away, trailing dust to mingle with the gunsmoke which drifted across Steele's side of the stalled Concord. But the cloud was not thick enough to blot out the scene. One brave was dead and another was writhing in agony as he clutched at the blood-gouting wound in his stomach. Then he, too, was still, as an exploding rifle

53

blasted a second bullet into his flesh: tearing through his back to find his heart.

The wounded pony and Mrs Lucifer were the only living things within range of the Colt Hartford now: the fat woman on her belly and clawing at the ground to which she had jumped as the first shots sounded. Until he made the half turn a complete one and threw himself full length beneath the Concord, thumbing back the hammer of the rifle.

The cloud of dust was thicker over the scene on the far side of the coach. Raised by the flailing legs of three wounded ponies who were down on their sides, pumping new spurts of dark crimson with each spasming movement of their struggle to get four-footed again.

One brave was slumped and inert. Two others were on their feet, drunken rage having displaced the shock on their raddled faces. Their Spencer rifles were levelled from their hips and their fingers were curled to the triggers.

Steele drew a bead on one of them and had taken first pressure against his own trigger: when his view was blocked by the flared skirts of three women plunging from the coach to the ground.

This in a space of a second of eerie silence – which was broken by a new fusillade of gunfire. The trio of whores collapsed to the ground amid fresh gunsmoke.

One of the Apaches staggered backwards two paces, a blood-bubbling hole between his nostrils and top lip and a blossoming stain on his right thigh. His Spencer, wisping grey smoke from the muzzle, fell from his hands and he followed it down.

The second brave had a bloody furrow across one cheek where a bullet had ploughed over the flesh without finding a hold. But the wound was enough to turn him, spoiling his aim. And Steele's rifle and a revolver fired in unison ensured he had no time to find a target again. He flung his arms high, hurling his cold rifle away. His mouth gaped wide enough so that every vein on his face and throat seemed to bulge against the underside of his filthy skin. But his scream became no more than a moist gurgle as blood from punctured lungs filled his windpipe and gushed over his lower lip. He sprawled on to his back, arms and legs still spread-eagled.

A new silence, broken by the snicker of a dying pony. Then small sounds as the Virginian backed out from beneath the coach and came erect. The sounds of weeping – from one of the whores pressing her trembling body to the ground and another still inside the Concord.

'Didn't I tell you!' Sally Swenson yelled in high delight. 'It isn't hard at all! Killing people who mean you harm!'

She was staring out through the shards of shattered glass still held in the window frame, her big, bright eyes fixed on the inert form of the Apache she had finished off with a bullet in the back.

On the seat opposite, Hope was triggered into a more violent fit of weeping by the shouted words, hiding her contorted face behind her hands.

'Like riding a horse,' Steele murmured as he cocked the Colt Hartford, levelled the rifle from his hip and exploded a bullet into the head of the wounded pony. 'Once you learn how, you never forget.'

Hope moved her hands from her face to her ears at the sound of the new shot. And kept her tear-reddened eyes tight shut. Two other women screamed.

He ignored all other sights and sounds except the agony of the three other injured ponies. Until he had emptied his own rifle to put two of them out of their misery, and used a discarded Spencer with a bloodstained stock to quieten the third.

'You're a good teacher, Adam,' Nancy Maguire said dully.

He had dropped the Spencer and tilted the Colt Hartford at the sky, to turn the cylinder and tip out the expended shell cases. Now he looked at the whore up on the Concord seat. She was still half sprawled across the seat, gripping the once-fired Colt loosely.

'But ain't much can happen to somebody learnin' to ride a horse. Some lumps and bruises or maybe a busted leg.' She shifted her saddened gaze from the impassive Virginian to the Apache she had helped to blast into eternity. 'Maybe all they really wanted was food and drink. And I figure I'm goin' to hurt real bad for killin' . . . '

'Nonsense!' Mrs Lucifer snapped as she stormed around the front of the uneasy team, vigorously dusting off her dress and patting her disarranged hair. 'We did what we had to do and we did it well. We must consider ourselves very lucky to have suffered no casualties.'

The younger women were evenly divided in their reactions to the violence. Sally Swenson, Gertrude and Faith were finding the taste of survival sweet. Hope, Charity and Nancy Maguire were to varying degrees revolted by the sprawled corpses of Apaches and crumpled carcasses of the ponies.

'Damn right!' Gertrude agreed vehemently, and smiled brightly at Steele as he fed fresh shells into the chambers of the Colt Hartford. 'And we have Adam Steele to thank for that.'

'It was no trouble, was it, Adam?' Nancy asked, pulling herself erect on the seat.

The Virginian concentrated his gaze on the reloading chore as he answered: 'It might have been. Did what was necessary to stop it if that was what it was going to be.'

'Easy as fallin' off a horse,' Nancy suggested dully.

'Or rolling in the hay,' the lone man among women countered. 'Each to what he does best, lady.'

Nancy looked at him again, with a glint of triumph in her eyes, as the rest of the women watched the exchange quizzically. 'I've never been ashamed of how I make a livin'.'

'Nor got tired of it either, I reckon,' Steele replied, resenting the feeling that he was on the defensive. 'Seeing as how you're always lying down on the job.'

Chapter Five

Only Mrs Lucifer felt insulted by Steele's jibe and she confined her response to a brief glower before she ordered the women to prepare to continue the trip west. This did not take long and within a few minutes the Concord was rolling again, the humped forms of dead animals and Apaches first veiled by trailing dust and then swallowed up by distance.

The Virginian rode out ahead, alone. With all the whores and the runaways back inside the coach and Mrs Lucifer up on the seat. Except for an irritating feeling of regret that he had allowed himself to take part in the exchange with Nancy Maguire, Steele was at peace with himself. The plan had worked well, the women had trusted him enough to do as he told them and there had been no doubts in his mind as the sound of the Colt Hartford cracked in his ears and the recoil jerked the stock-plate against his shoulder. And there were none now as he rode easily astride the gelding across the arid, seemingly endless scrub desert.

Back aboard the doomed riverboat he had made a mistake, because he was not perfect. Had fate decided he had suffered enough for the error, or had he simply been hardened still further? There would be other mistakes and maybe other innocents would spill their blood across his path or on his back trail. But that was life – and death – and something had happened to him since he met up with the women: so that once more he was able to accept such harsh realities without dwelling on the part he was allotted to play.

And all that bothered him as he signalled a halt for a midday rest and meal was the need he had felt to justify himself to a conscience-stricken whore.

As he took care of the horses while the women built a fire and prepared food, he saw that the memories of what had happened a little over two hours previously were already beginning to lose their vividness. Mrs Lucifer was as efficiently domineering as when he first saw her and the whores did her bidding with meek compliance. Recent triumphs no longer gave Sally Swenson confidence and she was afraid again – her big blue eyes constantly wandering from the task in hand to search the undisturbed horizon on all sides.

There was little unnecessary talk during the preparation and eating of the beef and beans meal. But no words were needed for the rest of the women to be infected by the runaway's nervousness. And as the coffee pot was passed around the changeabout was complete. Only Sally had been displaying her true feelings. The others, including the fat and ugly madam, had been harbouring dark fears behind wafer-thin veneers of normality.

'You must consider us complete fools, Mr Steele,' Mrs Lucifer said suddenly after a lengthy silence during which the women sipped their coffee as automatically as they had picked at their food.

'Why should I do that, ma'am?'

He was sitting with his back against a wheel, getting what benefit he could from the shadow of the coach under a sun just beyond its peak. The women were spread in a scattered group in front of him, apparently unmindful of the harsh heat beating down on their wide-brimmed hats.

'City women like us, not used to the dangers of the open country. Settin' out on such a journey without escorts.'

'Reckoned the people who ran you out of Houston didn't give you time to . . .'

'They gave us the choice of which way to head. We came west

58

on impulse. And people who act recklessly are foolish, wouldn't you say?'

Steele pursed his lips.

Nancy Maguire spoke first, after a deep sigh. 'If Adam was to say yes, he'd be callin' himself a fool, madam. He didn't do much thinkin' before he joined us.'

The old woman gestured with a pudgy hand to dismiss the side issue. Then looked hard into the shaded face of the Virginian. 'It's beside the point, but I'm sure Mr Steele never does anythin' without good reason.'

He acknowledged this with a nod. 'To stay alive.'

Nancy shook her head in denial. 'A thousand bucks ain't what's between you and the grave.'

'Starving's a bad way to die, I reckon.'

The rest of the women were not involved in the exchange: seemed not even to be listening. Sally maintained her survey of the distant heat shimmer while the others were alone in a crowd with their own dark thoughts. But Steele was conscious of their presence and aware of mounting irritation as he found himself on the defensive again. And he had to make an effort to remain outwardly composed in front of many pairs of eyes, most of them not even looking at him.

In fact, only Nancy Maguire was examining him closely. For Mrs Lucifer was too involved with her own anxieties to notice the subtle tightening of the skin across his jaw.

'It matters not why he chose to help us, my dear,' she said with feeling. 'He did so and has proved himself entirely capable. And it is more than we deserve after actin' so stupidly.'

The Virginian did not consciously express a tacit warning to the whore who was watching him. But she read something in his dark, bleak eyes which caused her to gulp back the words she intended to speak: and to turn her attention to Mrs Lucifer.

'What are you tryin' to say, madam?'

'That I am grateful,' she replied spontaneously. Then showed the impassive Virginian a wan smile. 'But that goes without sayin', doesn't it? Maybe I don't quite know what I want to . . . '

'Figure I do, madam,' Nancy cut in with a voice holding

something close to sadness. 'And Adam and me already covered that ground. When we was ridin' together before he spotted the Indians.'

She glanced at Steele, perhaps to get his permission to continue. Or maybe to see if he recalled the conversation as something more than mere words to pass the time. But he drained the mug of the last drops of tepid coffee and his eyes above the rim transmitted nothing.

'People shouldn't have to apologise to each other for what they are, madam,' she went on in the same tone. 'Because anyone who figures they're what they want to be is the biggest kind of fool there is. But it ain't easy for people like us. We're what we are and Adam's what he is. And we make excuses. Money's the easiest one.' She glanced again at Steele, but this time their gazes met for only part of a second. 'Which is the same thing as stayin' alive, I guess. But what the hell does it matter? People only get to be angels after they're dead. And there's precious few do that.'

She had talked her way back to confidence and was able to look openly at the Virginian without nervousness. 'Like we agreed, Adam. No one's free of the way they are and it ain't no use at all makin' excuses. On account that anyone with a lick of sense can figure things out for themselves.' A glance towards the madam now. 'Call us fancy names, but all we are are whores.'

Mrs Lucifer became as rigid and grim-faced as a preacher's wife who has heard an oath in church. But the younger woman hurried on, with the attention of the other whores now, before the madam could voice her shock.

'Everyone in Houston knew that's what we was. But they went along with the fancy name we called ourselves until the strait-laced ticket won the election and told the truth the rest had always known.

'So you're right, madam. We oughta be grateful that Adam joined us. And consider ourselves lucky we made it so far outta Houston without trouble. But he ain't no better than us and I don't figure he thinks he is. So you don't owe him nothin' except gratitude and the money you're gonna pay him. On account he's only doin' what he has to do.'

She had lost the interest of the other whores now. For Mrs Lucifer had recovered her composure after the moments of shock, so the threat of anger was gone.

'I'm through now,' Nancy announced mildly.

'Without calling me the right name?' the Virginian asked evenly, easing to his feet and still aware of a slight pain in his legs.

'You ain't got no illusions about yourself no more, Adam,' she replied flatly. 'But if you want to hear it spoke out loud, you're a natural born killer.'

Mrs Lucifer caught her breath. But the Virginian's expression and gait did not change by even part of a degree as he moved to his horse and stowed his mug back in the bedroll. Then, when he turned to face the women and discovered all of them were looking at him with nervous expectancy, he found the smile that spread across his face required no pretence.

'Easy, ladies,' he said evenly. 'I never did claim to be anything else.'

'Except to yourself,' Nancy said.

'Leave it!' Mrs Lucifer snapped, not trusting the Virginian's nonchalant acceptance of the younger woman's charge.

Nancy ignored her. 'You want to leave it there, Adam?'

'There's no place else to take it,' he answered, and swung up into the saddle.

She got to her feet and the lines of strain on her face were suddenly lost under a relaxed smile. 'It's good to have it out in the open, isn't it?'

'That's your business,' he countered, and managed wryness rather than cynicism without conscious effort. 'Mine is killing people – wherever they ask for it.'

Nancy accepted the comment in the manner it was spoken, merely adding an edge of grimness to her smile. But the other women had caught Mrs Lucifer's distrust of Steele's attitude and continued to be nervous as they broke the midday camp and climbed back into the Concord.

Throughout the cruel heat of the long afternoon and the welcome coolness of evening, the Virginian maintained his lonesome vigil ahead of the slow-moving coach. Mrs Lucifer twice declined offers from inside the vehicle and stayed up on the seat in control of the weary team. If there was talk among the whores and Sally Swenson, it was not loud enough to carry outside the shattered windows.

The sun was down and bright moonlight was casting long, deep shadows when the madam called: 'Don't you think it's time we looked for a place to stop, Mr Steele?'

The Virginian had ridden this country before, on the eastwards trip from Borderville to New Orleans. A time without trouble or doubts. One of the best of the bad times. But no match for now.

He knew they were in the Pecos valley and judged that the river would become visible as soon as they were through a gully that offered a way into a convoluted area of rocky ridges a mile ahead. If he was right, they would reach Fort Pepper in less than two hours.

'Soon!' he called back and glanced over his shoulder to see Mrs Lucifer nod in acknowledgement.

Then he reverted to his automatic surveillance of the terrain on all sides, at peace with the world but instantly ready to declare brutal war on it should his life or the lives he was being paid to protect be threatened. And, even more important, at peace with himself. He was a hired gun and now he accepted this: no longer resentful of the fact that a whore had forced him to face the truth. For truth, no matter who spoke it, could not be denied if a man was to hold on to his self-respect. Any man, doing whatever he had to do.

The gully was a dangerous place with steeply sloped sides and a hundred pockets of cover. The women aboard the coach saw this and breathed faster as their eyes raked the shadowy broken ground and the ragged skylines to either side: their imaginations peopling the dark places with the human instruments of sudden death.

Steele saw only what was there: acknowledging potential danger and poised to react to it.

Then they were through and the sounds of the Concord's progress reverted to a usual level beyond the confines of the rocky slopes. The Pecos was a distant thread of moon-silvered water, appearing and reappearing among intervening points of high ground. The lights of Fort Pepper gleamed atop one of these hills, two miles south west of the gully.

'Are those lights?' Mrs Lucifer asked, still tense from the eerie experience of passing along the gully. Or perhaps merely suspicious of this sure sign of human presence in the wilderness.

Women's heads appeared at the shattered windows of the Concord.

'An army fort, ma'am,' Steele supplied.

'Thank God. Will they allow us to stay the night there?'

'Reckon your only trouble will be in leaving,' the Virginian answered. 'Women are almost as rare as snow in this part of the country.'

'Wow!' Nancy Maguire exclaimed excitedly, and abruptly there was just one face visible at the window.

That of the wide-eyed and fearful Sally Swenson who remained fixed in an uncomfortable attitude, leaning far out to stare at the distant lights atop the hill.

Steel continued to hold the gelding to an easy pace, even though he had seen Mrs Lucifer take a tighter grip on the team reins: obviously anxious to reach Fort Pepper as soon as possible. But the madam made no complaint that the Virginian was showing more concern for the weary horses than drained women over the final stretch of country to the promise of safety.

The fort was built of adobe, its sun-bleached white walls sharply defined in the light of kerosene lamps and the moon. Steele was conscious of being watched from the top of the east facing outer wall, then spotted the glint of fieldglasses to prove his instinct.

'Gate's to the north!' a man yelled down as Steele and the Concord came close to the foot of the hill on which the fort was built.

Steele raised a hand in acknowledgement and veered the gelding to the right, circling the hill until he found the rutted track which led up to the already opened double gates. It was steep, rising a hundred feet in five hundred and he halted to allow the heavy Concord to draw level with him.

'Can you handle it, ma'am?' he asked.

Mrs Lucifer looked different. Homely rather than ugly. He realised the flattering light of the moon contributed something to this. But he had seen her up close at night before without noticing any change. And he decided it was an easing of inner tension which was mainly responsible. A new found confidence close to the protection of the fort, which could also be heard in her voice.

'I have admitted to acting recklessly, Mr Steele. But I am not a moron. Had I not felt competent to drive this vehicle I would certainly . . .'

'If it's no sweat for you, it's not for me, either,' he cut in, and turned his horse away to ride up the track.

The crest of the hill had been levelled by the brute strength of army labour. On three sides the ground fell away sharply from the foot of the wall, but there was a narrow flat strip outside the north wall and as Steele reached this, he saw the four men standing in the gateway. Two enlisted men with their rifles ported, a captain and a civilian.

'Evenin' to you, sir. Captain Wilmot, duty officer. Welcome to Fort Pepper. The stage is a long way off the regular routes.'

He was in his late twenties, a good-looking blond with freckles. His salute was as smart as his uniform. The two enlisted men were at least fifteen years his senior: tough-looking veterans showing signs of weariness – perhaps with the night sentry duty or maybe with life in general at the fort.

All the soldiers were tall and lean, which emphasised the flabby squatness of the civilian. He was close to sixty with grey hair and a pale complexion. He had soft hands. But although he obviously lacked physical strength, there was a blatant hint of toughness in his square-cut features dominated by clear, bright blue eyes.

'Adam Steele, Captain,' the Virginian responded, acknowledging the salute with a brief touch at his hat brim. 'Not a regular stage. Group of ladies heading west privately. All but the driver young.'

The enlisted men showed grins of anticipation and lost interest in Steele to concentrate their attention on the spot where the Concord would reappear.

The officer glanced quickly at them and became anxious. 'We don't have the proper facilities to accommodate women, sir.'

Steele swung gratefully out of the saddle and relished the fact that his legs protested only slightly as he stood on the ground.

'You know their names, young feller?' the civilian asked sharply. He was switching an eager gaze between the Virginian and the top of the track. 'Or maybe Sally ain't usin' her real name. An eighteen-year-old blonde girl. Pretty, and I don't say that just 'cause she's my daughter.'

He stared hard and long at Steele now: and received not a flicker of response from the impassive face. 'Be up here in a couple of minutes, feller,' the Virginian supplied. 'You can check them over for yourself. Seem to recall most of them are redheads.'

One of the enlisted men vented a low growl of pleasure.

'Come on, young feller,' Swenson snapped. 'If you've been ridin' with them, surely you must have taken more notice than that!'

'A whore is a whore is all,' Steele answered, and started to lead his horse around the line of men in the gateway.

'Didn't I tell you things had to get better, Austin?' one of the enlisted men blurted, his accent broadly Irish.

'Frig it, I'd better let Major Salk know the score!' Wilmot croaked. But in starting to whirl he saw the brightness of the grins on his men's faces. 'You're still on duty!' he snarled. 'Remember that or you won't be so happy when I haul the both of you up in front of the major at report.'

The men came sharply to attention, as impassive as Steele except for their eyes which continued to be eager and trained on the top of the track.

'Let the rig in and close up the gates!' Wilmot instructed. 'But don't allow nobody off until I've checked with the major.'

'Sir!' Austin acknowledged.

Wilmot completed his turn and started at a brisk walk – almost a march – across the compound. Swenson, looking crestfallen, moved at the same easy pace as Steele, his shoulders hunched and his hands deep in the pockets of his suit pants.

'Guess even Sally wouldn't tie in with a bunch of whores,' he growled, glanced at the Virginian and tried to talk up some interest from him. 'Name's Swenson, Steele. Run a small spread east of Houston. Just me and my daughter Sally. Eighteen years old and took it into her head to up and beat it. All on account of some no-good drifter. Left me in a real hole with stock to tend and fields to take care of. Not that that's my main concern, young feller. It's makin' sure Sally don't ruin her life that's my big worry.'

Steele did not have to look at Swenson a second time to confirm that the man was lying. If he had ever done any hard manual work it had been a long time ago. And his daughter was certainly the least hardy of all the women aboard the Concord.

'Your problem, feller,' the Virginian responded indifferently as he completed his survey of Fort Pepper.

He had seen it only from the outside at a distance on his eastward trip. Inside, it conformed to the pattern of other army posts he had entered in the south west. The high adobe walls with the timber walkways for the sentries to patrol. A hard-packed compound with a flag mast at the centre. Adobe buildings on three sides to house sleeping, living and working quarters for men and officers: plus a stable block and an armoury. He guessed it had an establishment of no more than thirty and saw from many signs of neglect that Major Salk was a sloppy commanding officer in at least one respect.

As Steele halted in front of the stable block, Swenson seemed about to snarl an angry retort to his unsympathetic comment. But he chose to express contempt instead.

'Guess you don't have any, young feller. With a bunch of whores to take care of you.'

'Other way around,' Steele answered, leaning against the rail to which he had hitched the reins. 'My job to take care of them.'

'Nice work if you can get it.'

The Virginian had pushed his hat on to the back of his head, so that the brim no longer threw moon shadow over his face. With a clear view of the hard-set features, Swenson seemed relieved that no offence had been taken at his remarks.

'It pays well,' Steele said evenly, as the heavy coach rolled through the gateway and the smartly turned-out Captain Wilmot emerged from a building accompanied by another man, hastily and half-dressed in uniform breeches and undershirt. 'Just money.'

Austin had halted the Concord at the gateway and exchanged a few words with the smiling Mrs Lucifer before allowing her to drive the heavy vehicle towards where the two officers were waiting. Both the enlisted men grinned broadly up at the broken windows as the coach rolled between them. But Mrs Lucifer had barked an order which ensured they received no vocal response from inside. Then they quickly closed and barred the gates and half-ran to catch up with the Concord.

As she drove by the stable block, the old woman interrupted her smile to direct a look at Steele, her expression heavy with secret meaning. Then she indicated Swenson with a fast movement of her eyes, and refixed the smile to her face for the benefit of the two officers.

The squat man was as intrigued by the Concord's passengers as the soldiers on the compound. Steele cast an apparently disinterested glance at them: enough to count just five women, with freshly made-up faces and recently brushed hair. Red hair, for Sally was not visible through the broken windows.

Up at the top of the walls, two sentries resumed their patrols, watching the surrounding hills and valleys. Austin and the other enlisted man on the compound took up rigid guard with their backs to the halted Concord. Wilmot was also deferential now that his commanding officer was present and Steele guessed that the lack of military orderliness at the fort was an indication of just one facet of Major Salk's way of running things. Another side of the man could be seen in his bloodshot eyes and the unsteadiness of his stance. He was tall and thin and on the wrong side of fifty, with a hollow-cheeked, heavy-browed, puckermouthed face. His hair was thinning and greying. The lobe of his left ear was missing. He was either still drunk or suffering the after effects of drinking.

'Captain Wilmot informs me you have a travelling whorehouse, madam,' he growled, making it a simple statement which he did not amplify by either tone or expression.

Mrs Lucifer wiped the smile off her face to glower towards

Steele. But she was calm again when she returned her attention to Salk.

'The captain was wrongly informed, major,' she responded, obviously pleased by the way the two officers tried to sneak surreptitious looks into the dark interior of the Concord. 'But if you will allow my ladies and I to spend the night here, I am sure we will be able to offer you and your men a pleasant respite from the monotony of life in this wilderness.'

'It's my duty to offer army hospitality,' Salk told her, no longer trying to conceal his curiosity about the women aboard the coach. 'You want to come on into my office and straighten me out on who I'm offering it to?'

'Be glad to, major.'

As she started to climb down, stiff and awkward from so many hot and uncomfortable hours on the hard seat, Wilmot hurried forward to help her. Mrs Lucifer's appreciation of the gallantry was almost girlishly coy.

'Well, are they whores or ain't they, Steele?' Swenson wanted to know.

'You pay your money and luck makes the choice,' the Virginian replied, turning his back on the curious man to begin unfastening the saddle cinch at the gelding's belly.

'You're a young feller of few words and them you say don't mean much.'

'Like a lady told me, we can't help being the way we are, feller.'

Certain now of a night at Fort Pepper, the Virginian swung open the stable door and led his mount inside. The place was clean and the cavalry horses looked fit and well cared for. There were four empty stalls and Steele talked the gelding into one of them. After supplying the animal with feed and water, he hung his saddle on a hook at the front of the stall, then sat on his bedroll and chewed on some jerked beef.

It was pleasantly warm in the stable as the night air outside grew colder. And the whole fort was quiet again after the disturbance caused by the entrance of the new arrivals. Steele enjoyed the peace and solitude, relishing the period of rest after the long, hot ride. He was conscious of mild hunger, sleepiness and the discomfort of old sweat and ingrained dirt.

Then footfalls and voices sounded outside, but he remained where he was. And was chewing a final piece of dried meat when the freckle-faced Wilmot halted in the open doorway.

'It seems we are in your debt, sir.'

'The women don't belong to me, captain.'

The uniformed figure advanced into the stable, his teeth gleaming in the filtered moonlight as he smiled. 'Some feminine entertainment will be very welcome, that's a fact. But I meant the Apaches. Mrs Lucifer told the major what happened. We've been hunting that bunch of renegades for weeks now.'

'All in the day's work.'

'Lieutenant Conway is out leading a patrol. He won't be back until tomorrow afternoon. You're welcome to use his quarters – if you don't mind sharing with Mr Swenson.'

'Grateful to you,' the Virginian said, easing to his feet and sliding the Colt Hartford out of the boot.

'We're having a meal prepared for the ladies. You'll join them, no doubt.' He brightened his smile into a grin. 'Seeing as how it's for ladies, maybe the post cook will fix something decent for a change.'

'I already ate.'

'Then I'll show you to Conway's quarters, sir.'

'Fine.'

They went out of the stable just as Austin reached the doorway, leading the four team horses. The Concord, now empty of its passengers, was parked beside two flatbed wagons at a far corner of the compound. The man who had been with Austin was now back at his post on the walkway to one side of the double gates. Although Fort Pepper was quiet again, there was a subtle atmosphere of excitement trapped between its high walls. Crossing the compound beside Wilmot, Steele sensed many pairs of eyes watching them and guessed that every man on the post had been roused to watch the women climb down from the coach and go out of sight.

'The Major's agreed to allow the ladies to put on a show for the men,' Wilmot said, discounting himself by his choice of words while his tone proved he was as eager as anyone to see what Satan's Daughters had in store. 'It'll be just the kind of morale-booster we've been needing. Not the easiest thing in the world, keeping soldiers at peak readiness in a place like this. Nearest town is fifteen miles south. And what they've got there isn't worth riding a half mile to see.'

'San Jose,' Steele said as they stepped up onto the stoop where Major Salk had first appeared.

'You know this part of the territory, sir?'

'Rode through it a while back,' the Virginian replied absently, his attention diverted by a movement at the parked Concord.

But there was nothing surreptitious in the attitude of Swenson as the short, fat man emerged from the shadows and strode purposefully across the compound towards the gates. There was a grim expression on his face and he appeared not to see Steele and Wilmot: or anything else that was not directly in his path.

'That feller been here long, Captain?'

Wilmot was unsettled by the sudden change of subject. He saw Swenson, just before Austin opened one of the gates to allow the civilian outside. 'Arrived this morning, sir. Claims to be looking for an errant daughter.'

'He told me.'

'This way, sir.'

They entered the building and Wilmot took the lead, along a narrow hallway lit by two kerosene lamps. There were several doors on either side and Mrs Lucifer's voice could be heard beyond one of them. Her words were indistinct, but her tone of authority was clear enough.

'This is it, sir. I hope you find it comfortable.' He pushed open a door and stood aside.

'Grateful to you, captain,' the Virginian said, crossed the threshold and glanced around the moonlit room. It was small, furnished with two narrow cots, a writing bureau and chair, a glass-fronted case crammed with military textbooks and a squat, unlit stove. The single window looked out over the compound. 'Be fine.'

'Then I'll leave you, sir.'

One of the neatly made cots had a pair of saddlebags stuffed under it. Steele dropped the Colt Hartford on to the other one.

And nodded. Wilmot saluted, closed the door and his footfalls retreated down the hallway. He halted for a few moments, and exchanged words with a woman. Then continued on his way.

Steele stretched out full length on the blanket-covered mattress and waited, enjoying the comfort of a bed under a roof for the first time since he slept aboard the *Queen of the River*. Fully dressed, he rested with fingers interlocked at the nape of his neck, peering up at the ceiling-hung kerosene lamp and listening to the rising volume of noise as Fort Pepper prepared for the promised pleasures of Satan's Daughters. Closer at hand was the pad of bare feet on the adobe floor of the hallway. Then the rap of knuckles on the door panel.

'It's open and I'm decent,' he called.

Nancy Maguire had started through the doorway as she knocked, without waiting for the invitation. She was dressed the same as when he had last seen her, except for boots and hat.

'Leave it open,' he instructed. 'Or the army might get the wrong idea.'

'Frig off, Adam!' she growled, and leaned against the door to close it. 'You ain't never worried about what other people think of you. All you gotta do is learn to live with yourself.'

'Reckon I'm getting close to top of that class. Didn't reckon it would be you paying me a visit.'

'Mrs Lucifer sent me. She give her word to Sally and she's real stubborn after she's done that.'

Nancy remained with her back to the door while the Virginian continued to rest easy on the bed.

'How did the girl know her Pa was at the fort?'

'She didn't. It's just that whenever we know we're gonna meet up with other people, she drops off the rig and hides until Mrs Lucifer gives her the all clear. Seems this time she was right to do it.'

'And what's right for me to do?'

A shrug of the shoulders. 'I'm just givin' you a message, Adam. Mrs Lucifer figures she hired you to protect all of us – including that crazy little rich bitch. Rest of us are safe enough, surrounded by army. Sally Swenson is outside someplace, hidin' behind a rock or somethin'. And she could be froze to death

71

come mornin'. End of message, Adam. I gotta get back now. Show'll be startin' soon.'

Reckon it'll be a sell out,' Steele said, swinging his feet to the floor as the woman pulled open the door.

'We won't be chargin' the army.'

'For anything?'

'There won't be anythin' but the show,' she replied bitterly. 'The friggin' major's friggin' order.'

'Maybe he'll change his mind when he's all dressed up and realises he is a major.'

'What?' she asked, puzzled, as she paused in the act of leaving the room.

'That he's the commanding officer here,' Steele drawled as he rose from the bed and canted the Colt Hartford to his left shoulder. 'Gives him the privilege of being first in the friggin' order.'

Chapter Six

There were more than twenty enlisted men and non-coms on the compound as Steele crossed to the gates, busy with building fires for warmth and light and arranging a double bank of chairs around an area encircling the flagpole. They worked cheerfully, in keen anticipation of the reward for their labours.

The Virginian was ignored until Trooper Austin came down from his sentry post on the wall to draw the bar from its brackets on the double gates.

'Hey, mister. Are them women whores or ain't they?'

'Matter of opinion, feller.'

The soldier's dark brown, deeply lined face took greater hold on its expression of frustration. 'But you been ridin' with them, mister. You must know.'

'Know one thing, feller,' Steele answered as one of the gates was opened wide enough for him to pass through the gap.

'What?'

'With these women, you've got two things going for you.'

'Yeah?' Austin was eager now.

'You wear pants and you've got something inside them.'

Austin grinned. 'Easy as that, uh?' Then his tone changed as Steele stepped outside the fort. 'Hey, what's with you and Swenson, mister? There ain't nothin' out there but rock, dust and cold. And white hatin' Apaches if you're that unlucky.'

'My kind of country,' the Virginian muttered as he started towards the edge of the hill's level top.

Austin grunted and closed the gate. This seemed to make the air colder and deepen the darkness of the moon shadows. The surrounding hills looked bleaker, the walls of the fort higher and more impregnable. So that the very atmosphere of night suddenly possessed a quality of eerie hostility.

'You lied to me, Steele!'

Swenson rasped the accusation as the Virginian reached the top of the track. He was sitting on a rock some fifteen feet below, aiming a cocked Army Colt towards the short, lean figure who had halted above him. He held the gun in a double handed grip, much as his daughter did, with the base of the butt clenched between his thighs.

'When was that, feller?' Steele asked evenly, his stance casual and his expression relaxed. The moon was behind the man below him and he could read nothing of the expression on the shadowed face.

'Sally was aboard that rig. Her valise is in the boot. Mono-grammed special the way I had done before I give it to her on her last birthday.'

'I say she wasn't?'

'You didn't say she was, Steele!'

'You reckoned your daughter wouldn't ride with whores. Why you pointing a gun at me, feller?'

Swenson's teeth gleamed in a silent snarl. 'Sally's out here someplace. I couldn't be sure of that until you came out. She could have left them anywhere. But you didn't come out for fresh air.'

'Nor to have a gun pointed at me, feller.'

'You know why Sally's run away from home, Steele?'

'You told me. To marry a feller you don't like.'

There was a pause. 'Yeah, I did tell you. That's right. You ain't married? You don't have no kids?'

The fires in the compound were alight and blazing, the flames reaching high to spread a glow of colour in the night. Suddenly there was a burst of applause – hand clapping, whistling and cheering.

'Something I've already told you, feller. Your problems aren't mine.'

'So don't try to understand!' Swenson snarled. 'It goes a hell of a lot further than runnin' off to hitch herself to some no-good drifter. Sally sure wouldn't have told you that. And it sure ain't no good me tryin' to appeal to you. So I'm right to have this gun on you, Steele! And I'll damn well use it if I have to.'

'What do I have to do to stop that happening, feller?'

'Drop the rifle and wait. It's cold and it's gonna get a hell of a lot colder. And I figure we can take that better than Sally can. Sooner or later she'll have to come up to the fort. If she don't want to die from exposure.'

Behind the walls of Fort Pepper, Satan's Daughters were staging their show. One of them was singing, high and clear, to the accompaniment of a lower keyed counterpoint provided by the others. Something from the classics, vaguely familiar to Steele: from bygone days on the Virginia plantation.

'Way I've seen it, she could prefer dying that way than going home with you, feller.'

Swenson made a sound of despair. But instantly brought his emotions under control. 'And maybe I'd prefer her dead than doin' what she is. Drop the gun, Steele!'

Austin and another trooper were up on the north wall walkway, either side of the gates. Even if they were able to tear their attention away from the women, though, to maintain their duty watch on the surrounding terrain, they would not have seen Swenson. Nor heard the talk above the singing of the women. They would just have seen the Virginian standing nonchalantly at the top of the track, apparently taking the cold night air. And his actions of stooping to lay the rifle on the ground, then coming erect again to start down the track might have appeared odd. But not suspicious.

'What the hell?' Swenson growled, half rising from the rock and pushing the Colt far out in front of him as Steele advanced.

'Takes a long time for somebody to die of the cold, feller. And I've had a long day.'

There were several rocks scattered to the side of the track. Steele chose one four feet away from where Swenson sat, and lowered himself on to it. He pulled his hat brim down lower and turned up the collar of his suit jacket. Then appeared to relax again. The older man remained tense and Steele tried to recall a time when he would have felt sympathy for Swenson. But it was too long ago across years and experience. And he simply regarded him as a pathetic fool: suffering from stupidity that invited death but did not deserve it. So the Virginian had not killed the man when he had the chance – as he stooped and swung down the Colt Hartford to rest it on the ground. And he waited now only for an opportunity to disarm him without hurting more than his feelings.

'I've been a fool far as that girl's concerned,' Swenson growled.

'Just thinking the same thing, feller.'

The older man grimaced. 'Give her too much of everythin'. Includin' freedom. And she took me for everythin'. Why, if I had to do . . .'

It was as if Swenson had fallen under the influence of the sadly sweet music filtering down from the fort at the top of the hill. His expression had become melancholy and his tone maudlin.

Steele appeared to be toying with his upturned jacket lapel, apparently indifferent to the other man. Until Swenson made the mistake of allowing his attention to wander away from the Virginian – his gaze seeking some visible sign of Sally's presence in the moon-shadowed valleys between the hills. It was then that Steele's hand wrenched away from his neck.

Swenson heard the faint rustle of silk against the coarser fabric of the jacket: but turned too sharply as he vented a low cry of alarm. The speed of the move unbalanced him on the rock and the Colt was jolted off target. His eyes widened with fear as he saw the Virginian, powering upright with something long and pale coloured extending from his hand. The younger man leaned closer to the older one and the scarf curved and coiled, one of the weighted corners dragging it around the wrist of Swenson's gun hand.

Steele leaned backwards, jerking at the scarf. Swenson's fear expanded and his mouth gaped so that his lips seemed to dis-

76

appear. He was wrenched up from the rock and half turned by the perfectly balanced, brute strength of the compactly built Virginian. The big Colt dropped from his hand as a bolt of pain shot from his constricted wrist to splay his fingers.

A vocal response to agony and fear began as a wet sound deep in his throat. But was trapped there as a gloved fist slammed into his jaw. His mouth snapped shut with a sharp crack of teeth coming together. And he dropped hard to his knees.

Steele kicked the discarded gun away and it skittered through the scattering of rocks.

Up at the fort, raucous applause greeted the end of the song. Then a harmonica whined, building up the tempo, and was joined by a trio of women's voices in a rousing sea shanty.

Steele slackened the scarf and pulled it gently so that it unwrapped from around the wrist. Swenson remained on his knees, tears of pain and frustration coursing his bulbous cheeks as he massaged the whole length of his forearm.

'Here's what you are going to do, feller,' the Virginian said evenly, replacing the damaging scarf loosely around his neck. 'You're going up to the fort, saddle your horse and ride.'

'You sneaky bastard!' Swenson accused, and groaned as his jaw seemed to catch fire with the opening of his mouth.

'Hurts to talk, uh? No sweat. You don't need to speak to anyone. The army's got plenty to keep it occupied right now. Won't even notice you ...'

'It's my money she's payin' you!' Swenson growled. 'If you're gettin' money as well as her.'

'Just do like I told you, feller,' Steele countered. 'And remember something. If I see you again before my job's over, it will hurt you more than it does me.'

He turned his back on Swenson, to go to the top of the track and pick up his rifle.

'I'll double whatever you're bein' paid, Steele!'

The squat Swenson was on his feet, having to splay his legs wide to remain upright as he recovered from the fall and the punch.

'I couldn't afford it, feller,' Steele answered, canting the Colt

77

Hartford to his left shoulder and having to raise his voice as the soldiers joined in the chorus of the song.

'What the hell is that supposed to mean?'

'I'm almost out of principles. Can't afford to sell out any more.'

Swenson used a coat sleeve to brush the tears from his face. And in the same action he formed his features into an expression of contempt. 'Them you got left stink, mister!' he snarled as he started up the track.

Steele nodded and showed a cold grin. 'Lots of people have said I come a little high.'

Chapter Seven

The Virginian watched Swenson ride in a half circle around the base of the hill and then head south on the well-used supply trail to San Jose. He had remained outside the fort while the older man was preparing to leave and if anybody apart from the two gate sentries had noticed his departure, it had not interrupted the giving and the enjoying of the show.

Steele watched the diminishing figures of the horse and rider from a corner of the fort, until they went from sight behind the opposite corner. Then he returned to the top of the track, raised the Colt Hartford high in the air and swung it from side to side. His impassive gaze raked the terrain and spotted Swenson's errant daughter the moment she showed herself, rising stiffly to her feet at the brow of a rise a half mile north east of Fort Pepper.

It took her a long time to cover the intervening distance. But although her walk became more fluid as the exercise eased muscles cramped by inertia, she was still trembling violently as she came to a halt beside Steele. She wore only the unflattering dress and whatever was underneath it. And the pale skin of her face and hands was pinched blue by the cold of the night air. She had to control the chattering of her teeth before she could speak.

'He knew I was out there, didn't he?' She crossed her arms in front of her small breasts and gripped her shoulders.

'That's right.'

'How?' She worked some hatred into her big eyes. 'Who told him?'

'Something from a time better than this.' He nodded for her to continue on into the fort. 'Birthday present with your initials on it.'

'Shit!' she hissed through clenched teeth. 'Why'd you let him get close enough to the rig to see that!'

'I'm in the bodyguard business,' Steele told her, nodding for her to move forward again after she had halted to hurl the words back at him. 'For taking care of property there'd be another charge.'

'He won't go far. He'll trail us. Or maybe he'll get some help.'

'Got the impression your Pa's the kind of feller who doesn't give up easily,' he allowed, moving ahead of her to push open the gate.

For some minutes the harmonica music had been soft and low key, with a subtle hint of the sensuous. There was no singing and the audience had been totally silent. Even the sentries up on the walls had been held as if spellbound by what was happening on the firelit compound below them: not casting the briefest of glances towards the shadowed hills and valleys it was their duty to watch.

Now, as Steele moved through the gap in the gates behind Sally Swenson, he saw the erotic reason for the men's avid attentiveness.

Mrs Lucifer, dressed in an elaborately lace-trimmed gown of flame red, was crouched on one of the adobe blocks surrounding the base of the flagpole. It was she who played the harmonica, the gentle waves of music perfectly complementing the performance of the younger women.

They were dancing, their bodies and limbs moving in slow time as they circled her: each of them facing a section of the rapt audience. Their gowns were also flame red, but without concealing trim: fitting skin tight from throat to belly then hanging loosely and split from crotch to hem. Thus, as the women moved, watching eyes caught tantalising glimpses of long legs clad in black fishnet hose: adding further to the arousal of sex-starved men already lusting for the jutting breasts explicitly contoured by the clinging fabric.

The faces of the dancers were expertly made up to accentuate individual attractive features and the expressions they wore were equally as professionally expert. For Nancy, Faith, Hope, Charity and Gertrude were conveying the same degree of lustful want as the men who drank in the sight of them.

Steele caught himself in the act of being stirred by what he saw: and sought to dampen his feelings by generating admiration for the idea behind the performance rather than what he was watching. It was at once obscene and yet filled with artistry, this combination somehow holding the men tensely on their seats, wide eyed and silent.

Then a single slight movement outside the circle of erotic dancers caught Steele's attention and he did a double take at Major Salk. Fully dressed now, the commanding officer of the post was drinking again: constantly raising the bottle of liquor, taking a swig and lowering it. And, while the other men were content to feast their eyes on each woman that writhed into their range of vision, Salk concentrated entirely on Gertrude – the tallest of the dancers by three inches and the one with the fullest figure.

The four fires were still burning brightly, their warmth extending all the way to the walls of the fort. Sally Swenson had stopped shivering from the cold, but her lower lip quivered as she looked in the same direction as Steele and sensed the prelude to evil.

'I sure hope the girls know what they're doing,' she whispered, and sidled closer to the Virginian, nervously conscious that the two troopers on the north wall kept allowing their attention to stray to her. 'This isn't Houston with a bunch of strong arm helpers close by in case of trouble.'

'You've seen it before?' Steele asked, switching his gaze briefly to Captain Wilmot. The freckle-faced junior officer was now only pretending an interest in the lewd dance. He was more concerned with the heavy drinking and single-minded pre-occupation of Salk.

'No, but they told me about it. Up until now they've always put on their show in saloons and dancehalls or at private parties. There never was trouble because whoever was paying them used to hire guards. Oh, no . . . !'

Salk had drained the bottle and it was his act of rising from his chair that triggered the exclamation from Sally. Nancy Maguire, immediately in front of the major, and Faith and Gertrude on either side of her, came to an abrupt halt. Fear wiped the sensuality from their faces and froze them into rigidity. Men and women who had failed to see the tall major get unsteadily to his feet were forced into an awareness that something was wrong by the change which overcame the three dancers.

Every soldier swung his gaze towards Salk, angry or puzzled by the interruption. Faith and Hope cut their dance in mid-step. The music played on, for Mrs Lucifer's eyes were screwed tight closed above her hands wrapped around the harmonica.

'Sir!' Wilmot yelled, leaping to his feet beside Major Salk.

The senior officer raised his arm, hand fisted around the neck of the empty bottle. Wilmot instinctively leaned away from him. But Salk did not aim a blow: instead, he hurled his arm forward and released the bottle so that it smashed into a thousand fire glinting shards against an adobe block at the base of the flagpole.

A woman screamed. Not Gertrude, who seemed petrified by the power of Salk's stare which remained fixed upon her.

Mrs Lucifer snatched the harmonica away from her lips and snapped open her eyes. 'Major!' she shrieked. 'You gave me your word there would be no . . . '

'Button your friggin' mouth, lady!' Salk snarled, tugging at his incomplete left ear while his eyes continued to stare lustfully at the full-bodied Gertrude. 'You're talkin' to a man who ain't seen this much of a woman for more than a year. So I'm sure not gonna get all roused up without doin' somethin' about it!'

'We ain't ready for no single bunk sleepin' either, major!' a thick-set sergeant yelled.

'Damn right!' another man called hoarsely. 'We all been prick-teased too far for that!'

'And the civilian's been out and rustled up another of them, sir!' Trooper Austin bellowed above the barrage of voices raised in agreement.

As all eyes except those of Salk swung towards Sally Swenson and the Virginian, Satan's Daughters backed into a tight-knit group around Mrs Lucifer. Only the kind of man who was aroused by a cringing and helpless woman would have lusted after them now. Or a soldier who had not seen a woman for week after gruelling week at an isolated army post. For even their costumes had lost their appeal. Instead, in combination with the terror inscribed on their painted faces and the way in which they huddled together for mutual comfort, the revealing fit and cut of their gowns served only to strengthen the aura of pathetic misery generated by their position.

Steele waited patiently, ignoring the hand of Sally as it fastened a firm grip on his forearm. For there was still a chance that Major Salk would deny his men the pleasure he was set on enjoying himself. And another chance that they would obey his orders.

The shouting ceased and there was a brief, tense silence. The only sounds were from the crackling fires as all eyes swept their gaze to the fort's commanding officer. In the expectant stillness, liquor and lust acted to roughen and slur his voice even more.

'The one with the big tits is mine.' He took an unsteady step towards where Gertrude was pressed between Mrs Lucifer and Nancy Maguire. 'You men share the rest of 'em!'

'Yiiipppeee!' a voice yelled, piercingly shrill.

And the men surged forward, kicking over chairs and swinging at each other in their eagerness to stake first claims.

'Sir!' Wilmot roared, his youthful features contorted by indecision.

Some of the women screamed. As terrified as the rest in the face of the advancing troopers, Nancy Maguire compressed her lips into a tight line and directed her eyes towards Steele. The expression they held was of mild regret – almost as if she felt sorry for him. Then she gave a violent shake of her head: as he shrugged out of Sally Swenson's grip to whip the Colt Hartford barrel down into his free hand. His left thumb cocked the hammer while the rifle was moving. And his index finger squeezed the trigger the instant the gun was in a double handed grip.

The report of the rifle stilled every voice: and swung every head towards Steele. The bullet, aimed high into the air, fell to the distant ground beyond the fort. Sally Swenson gasped and backed rapidly away from the Virginian, anxiously eager to disassociate herself from him now that he was the centre of powerful attention.

For part of a second, Steele ignored everybody but Captain Wilmot: to stare at him with cold eyes in a face that conveyed no glimmer of what he was thinking. And his features did not alter their set by a degree as he swivelled his gaze the merest fraction to look at Salk.

'Tonight you're drunk, major,' he said evenly against the background noise of crackling fires. 'You'll be sober tomorrow.'

The commanding officer's thin face was blotchy from drinking and his eyes were bloodshot. His features were set in an expression of brutal lust, which easily transformed into hard anger.

'Guards!' he roared. 'Arrest that Goddamn civilian!'

Only the sentries on the walkways were armed with rifles. As duty officer, Wilmot wore his cavalry gunbelt with a revolver in the buttoned-down holster. Four Springfield rifles were angled down at Steele and triumphant smiles dissipated the shock from many faces. The women huddled closer together at the base of the flagpole.

Steele eased the Colt Hartford back to his shoulder and again looked at Wilmot. The young captain had got as far as unfastening the flap of his holster. But was hesitating, still undecided: and desperately afraid of his responsibilities.

'Drop the rifle, mister!' Austin snarled.

'No!' Wilmot countered, and grimaced at the odd shrillness of his tone. His hand shook as he raised the Colt; but became rock steady when he pressed the muzzle into the nape of Salk's neck. The freckles of his face stood out more clearly against his suddenly pale skin. And a hard tone of authority powered his words. 'I'm arresting the major! On a charge of drunkenness while in command of this fort.'

Salk had become as rigid as a stone statue when the gun muzzle touched his flesh. Except for his thin face, which expressed shock and horror before reverting to rage.

'You're friggin' what, captain?' he snarled.

Everybody saw he was on the point of powering into a whirl: to wrench himself away from the touch of the gun and display the ugliness of his feelings toward Wilmot.

But the junior officer matched Salk's tone and the words he spoke held no tremor of nervous bluff. 'You move a muscle until I tell you, major, and your brains'll be spread all over the compound.'

Now it was Salk who suffered an agony of indecision, his bloodshot eyes darting back and forth in their sockets to rake the faces of his men. His mind was still fuddled by alcohol, but he was sobering up fast. And realised that he was alone in a crowd. In the same way that Wilmot was also cut off from the men and women on all sides.

For, in the expressions of his men, he saw a willingness for him to beat Wilmot's play – but no offer of help. They were soldiers, accustomed to living by the dictates of the chain of command: in the habit of having responsibility carried by officers. They wanted their way with the women, but since they were on active duty at a military post, such pleasures had to have the approval of their commanding officer. And just who was in command was not clear-cut.

'This is mutiny, Wilmot!' the major said at length, breaking a long pause with a voice that shook. Perhaps from anger or fear or a combination of both. 'I'll see you court-martialled and . . .'

'You'll return to your quarters, major!' Wilmot cut in on him. 'Where you'll be confined under guard until I receive instructions from Department Headquarters. Move, sir!'

He leaned closer to Salk, pushing the gun muzzled harder into the man's neck. Salk scanned the faces of his men again and saw only regret.

'Sergeant Gillett!' Wilmot snapped. 'Assign three men and

arm yourselves. I want a round-the-clock guard on Major Salk!'

'Sir,' a tall, broad-shouldered non-com with a black beard growled savagely: and gestured with his head at three troopers close to him.

Salk watched the four men start towards the bunkhouse and their action seemed to drain from him the will to resist. He submitted to the pressure of the gun at his head and started forward. His lips moved, too, as he vented low curses, his features contorted into a look of vicious hatred.

Steele shifted his cold gaze from the two officers to rake the walkways at the top of the wall. Each man on duty up there sensed the survey and self-consciously ported his rifle to remove the last vestige of the overt threat against the Virginian. But resentment began to build in the cooling air as the fires burned low. Directed towards Steele, Captain Wilmot and the women. And perhaps some of it was turned inwards as the men mentally berated themselves for failing to support their deposed commanding officer.

'All right, you guys!' Nancy Maguire called shrilly, stepping away from the group. She stood with one hosed leg jutting out from the split in her gown, her hands fisted on her hips and her breasts thrust forward. 'If you're ready to wait your turns and treat us like ladies, you're welcome to have what you been missin' so long.'

There was another abrupt change of mood, as drastic as when Steele had exploded the shot into the air. Sexually frustrated men stared incredulously towards the suggestively posed and broadly smiling Nancy. And were roused again, their want expanding as Mrs Lucifer – smiling benignly – urged the other four women to display their wares.

Salk and Wilmot had almost reached the stoop of the building they were heading for: and the captain was forced to match the action of the major in coming to an abrupt halt. Salk backed away two steps, switching his again angry gaze between the women and Wilmot.

'See what you done, captain!' he snarled triumphantly. 'You put your friggin' career on the line for a bunch of friggin' whores! I knew what they were! Every man here knew! Except you, you crazy sonofabitch! Women don't do what they done unless they're ready to . . . '

'Halt or I'll fire!' Wilmot roared.

The major looked drunk again, eyes gleaming, and skin blotchy, his gait wavering as he lunged from in front of the aimed Colt: ignoring it as it swung to draw a bead on him in his rush towards Gertrude.

'Come on, you big, beautiful . . . '

The Colt bucked in Wilmot's hand. Salk had covered ten feet of ground when the shot rang out. He was stopped in mid-stride and as his leading foot slammed down it seemed as if the bullet burrowing into his back would pitch him forward. But he managed to retain his balance – until he raised his arms and stretched them out towards the horrified Gertrude who was still the sole object of his fixed gaze. He went down then, blood from a punctured lung cascading over his lower lip. His arms became limp in death and folded laxly under the weight of his inert body. He lay as still as the ground on which he rested.

Just for a second, Captain Wilmot lost his nerve, terrified by the act he had committed and its inevitable repercussions. But only the Virginian saw this, without having time to experience any sense of affinity with the freckle-faced youngster. For then the brief moment was gone and Wilmot was in full control of himself as all other eyes shifted from the dead man to him.

'This is an army post!' he snarled. 'And it's going to be run like one from now on! Sergeant Gillett and his squad will bury the major! All other troopers not assigned duties will return to their cots! The civilians will go to their quarters and remain there until morning, when they will leave!'

His head swung from side to side, treating each man and woman on the compound or up on the walkways to a hard-eyed glare of determination. The women by the flagpole were at first indignant, then meekly subservient. The men were once more resentful.

'But, captain, we are willin' to . . . ' Mrs Lucifer started as the women around her eased out of their inviting postures.

'Ma'am!' Wilmot interrupted. 'For too long the commanding officer treated Fort Pepper as a saloon. I have now replaced him and I do not intend for this post to become a whorehouse. Even for one night. You will now obey my orders – all of you!'

Again he raked his gaze over every face. There were, perhaps, two full seconds when nobody responded. Then a trooper angrily snatched up a chair and started towards the bunkhouse. Others followed him, giving the women a wide berth. Sergeant Gillett and his three man squad advanced on the corpse of Salk.

'Come, ladies,' Mrs Lucifer rasped. 'We owe it to the captain to do as he asks.'

She gestured with open palms to usher the women ahead of her towards their quarters.

'And I owe you, Mr Steele,' Sally Swenson said, still nervous, as she moved to his side again. 'For running off my father.'

The Virginian looked into her elfinly pretty face, but saw no implied meaning behind the words she spoke. 'There's no debt,' he told her. 'Mrs Lucifer's footing the bill.'

'Thanks, anyway,' she said, and hurried across the compound to catch up with the other women.

Steele followed at a more leisurely pace, ejecting the spent shellcase from the rifle and loading the chamber with a fresh round. The young captain continued to stand near the stoop, the revolver clutched tightly in his fist at the end of a loosely hanging arm. He watched the corpse of Major Salk until it was carried out of sight behind the armoury. There was a look of grim satisfaction on his freckled face.

'He was drunk more than he was sober,' Wilmot said softly as Steele drew close. 'And the worse kind of commanding officer all the time. There's not a man on this post who won't be glad he's gone – after they've forgotten what they missed out on tonight.'

'Reckon the army won't ever forget you didn't miss, captain,' the Virginian answered.

Wilmot shrugged and seemed suddenly to become aware that he was still holding the Colt. He holstered it and buttoned the flap. 'That's what being in command is all about, isn't it, sir? Making the decisions and being prepared to face the consequences.'

He gazed down at the patch of blood coughed up by the dying

Salk – an insignificant dark stain on the pale dust in the fading light of the almost burnt out fires. He continued to be satisfied with the outcome of the night's events and Steele now had the time to feel an affinity with him.

'So long as you're happy, captain.'

Wilmot looked up and nodded. 'I am, sir. And grateful to you for forcing me to do what was necessary.'

Steele shook his head. 'We're even. I'm responsible for the women. But you took the major decision.'

Chapter Eight

They left Fort Pepper as the sun was rising on a new day. They were washed up and had full bellies. Steele rode out ahead of the Concord in which the whores and the runaway were closeted, primly attired in their shapeless day dresses. Every trooper was on duty, those not assigned to the walkways busily engaged in bringing neatness and order to the fort. They watched the departure with sullen eyes, bitterly recalling the two lost opportunities of the previous night.

But no feelings were voiced, each man conscious of the stoic Captain Wilmot who stood at the open window of the late major's office. And it was left to the two troopers manning the gates to express an unsubtle and unspoken comment to demonstrate what the others were thinking. At the moment the horses hitched to the rear of the coach were clear of the entrance, they slammed the gates closed with violent intent. The sliding of the bar through the brackets was completed with just as much noisy emphasis.

Mrs Lucifer waited until they had reached the base of the hill and were rolling westwards again before she called out to Steele: 'I never considered the United States Cavalry would act in such a way!'

The Virginian looked back over his shoulder. 'What *did* you expect, ma'am?' he asked wearily.

'That an officer and so called gentleman would keep his word, sir!' She made a throaty sound of disgust, almost as if she intended to spit. 'He gave me his solemn promise that he would keep his men under control. And he could not even control his own animal desires!'

'Yeah, and we had them all eatin' outta our hands before that bum went crazy for Gertrude!' Nancy moaned from inside the Concord. 'And even after he got what was comin' to him, we could've showed those soldier boys a real time. If it hadn't been for that snotnose punk of a captain.'

There were sounds of agreement as Steele faced front again and began his involuntary survey of the terrain. He was not surprised to discover that he felt no anger for Nancy Maguire, who was totally unconcerned that her actions and words of the previous night had caused the death of Major Salk. And he simply told himself to stop searching his mind for responses that were not there any more.

'Never mind, ladies,' he heard Mrs Lucifer say. 'We are exploring unknown territory and must learn by our mistakes. Next time we will know better.'

They crossed the Pecos River at early evening when the sun was still harshly yellow as its leading arc touched the western horizon. It was an easy and uneventful crossing, which was in keeping with the entire journey from Fort Pepper. They had rested only briefly for a midday meal and Steele had dictated a pace that kept the animals reasonably fresh. The women had suffered, though, aboard the heavily laden Concord that rocked and jolted across rough, sun-baked country that threatened to break a wheel at every turn of the rim. During the break the cold meal had been eaten in near silence, the Virginian sitting apart and maintaining his vigil on the arid hill and desert country while the women suffered a delayed reaction to the events of the night. What desultory talk there was also excluded Sally Swenson who sat at a distance from the group, considering the immediate past only insomuch as it had a bearing on the future.

When they started moving again, Steele continued to spot familiar landmarks as he back-tracked on the way he had headed east. But then, beyond the Pecos, he had to deviate from familiar ground to find a route through the rugged wilderness for the lumbering Concord. And he discovered that he experienced a sense of relief when he had left behind this tenuous physical link with the past.

At night camp in a thick clump of mesquite and low brush beside a trickle of a stream which fed the Pecos, Faith and Hope built a fire and cooked a supper of beef stew and beans. Relieved by the coolness of evening and then the gentle warmth of the fire which kept the cold of night at bay, the women eased their aching bodies and felt the mental tension drain from their minds. They readily agreed to Steele's order that two guards be posted on points of high ground to the east and south of the camp and, while Sally Swenson and Hope stood the first watch, the others talked. About Houston and the trouble-free time there before the new administration ran them out of town. Mostly they retold stories of the good times, often glancing at Steele for a reaction to comic incidents. But he made no contribution until Gertrude asked directly of him:

'You think we're nuts, don't you, Adam? Tryin' to bring city-style entertainment to the backwoods?'

He was lying on a patch of tough grass, his head on his saddle. The women were all seated on their bedrolls.

'I reckon you'll do whatever the hell you want to,' he replied evenly without moving. 'For as long as you stay lucky.'

'You don't strike me as the kind of feller who sets store by luck,' Nancy countered.

Now he showed a cold smile. 'Okay, until the law of averages goes against you.'

Mrs Lucifer cleared her throat. 'We are not so naïve as you appear to think us, Mr Steele,' she said harshly. Then moderated her tone. 'Perhaps we were, when we made the impulsive decision to come west. But we have learned from every experience along the way. We have just been recallin' Houston, but we have no illusions about those times returnin'. Unless we can get to San Francisco or maybe Denver. Until then, we will continue to perform before any audience which wishes to see us. But we will trust no man's word and if we cannot hire guards, we will take steps to protect ourselves.'

92

'We made a pretty good job of that when the Apaches showed up,' Charity recalled.

'And we could've handled the soldier boys easy if it hadn't been for that liquored up major!' Faith added.

They looked expectantly at the Virginian, again waiting for a response. But he remained silent and impassive.

'I would say that Mr Steele is unimpressed, ladies,' Mrs Lucifer pronounced sourly.

'Not so, madam,' Nancy Maguire corrected. 'I think we've made quite an impression on him. Right, Adam?'

She looked at him knowingly.

'Reckon you'll be easy to forget,' he answered.

'Thanks a bunch!' Gertrude growled.

'On account of I'm always running into new trouble after the old kind has gone.'

'Bullshit!' Nancy snapped, and received a glower from Mrs Lucifer. 'He won't forget us in a hurry.'

As if to counter both sides of the disagreement, that night and the following two days and nights were uneventful. The world outside ignored the progress of the seven women and one man as they moved sedately across the arid terrain of southern New Mexico Territory. And there were no ill-tempered incidents sparked within the group to ripple the calm surface of their relationships.

The discomforts of the long trek continued unabated, but the city-bred women had had time to adjust to the dust and sweat and flies of the day and the chilling cold of night. And they accepted their self-imposed lot with less and less muttered complaints as each day passed.

But they did not allow themselves to be lulled into a false sense of security. They rode in the coach and slept in their bedrolls with rifles and revolvers always close to hand. And stood their periods of guard fully alert. Impressed by the Virginian's constant vigilance and with memories of recent violence fresh in their minds.

It was on the western slopes of the San Andre Mountains that trouble threatened once more. The time was a little after midday and the morning cloud cover had been dissipated without shedding any rain. The sun was harshly hot, forming the familiar heat shimmer and glistening mirages of non-existent lakes. It was in one of these tantalising images of a body of water that Steele thought he saw a glint of sunlight on shiny metal.

It showed as he rounded a high outcrop of rock at the end of a steep sided defile.

'Hold it up!' he shouted to Mrs Lucifer, who hauled on the reins to halt the team without sensing trouble.

Often, as they crossed the low but ruggedly sculptured mountains, a rockfall or gaping crevice had blocked their intended path and forced a back-track to find another route. And there was nothing in the Virginian's tone or attitude now to suggest this was not simply another occasion when they would have to make a detour. And the Concord was still twenty yards back in the defile, enclosed on two sides by high cliff faces and with the view ahead blocked by the outcrop.

The fat woman up on the box seat of the coach waited patiently, watching the back of Steele as he swung his head from side to side, scanning the panorama of the Rio Grande valley spread out before him. For several seconds the water mirage was undisturbed, except by the rippling effect of the shimmer. Then he saw the metallic glint again, and concentrated his attention on the distant spot. A few more seconds elapsed and four riders appeared in the haze: dark silhouettes with blurred outlines, bobbing up and down as the horses cantered. Perhaps two miles away, with flashes of reflected sunlight lancing away from more than one point now.

'Well, can we get through, or can't we?' Mrs Lucifer demanded. And there was both anxiety and irritation in her tone. Sunlight did not penetrate to the bottom of the defile, but the high walls acted to trap the still, pore-opening heat of morning. The deep shade seemed to emphasise the discomfort and while this caused her ill-temper, the ugly madam was also troubled that Steele was taking an uncommonly long time to make a decision.

The Virginian did not turn in the saddle. The riders below were galloping their mounts now and, much as had happened when the Apaches closed in, the dust they raised smudged the heat shimmer and made them even more indistinct. But he knew they could see him clearly, an unmoving figure against the sun-bleached outcrop.

'Company's coming,' he answered. 'Four white men riding fast. You want to try my way or yours?'

The news triggered a babble of competing voices from inside the Concord.

'Be quiet, ladies!' Mrs Lucifer ordered.

There was a moment of silence, then Sally called tensely: 'Is it my father?'

'It could be anybody.' He glanced coldly back at Mrs Lucifer, his coal black eyes and pursed lips demanding an answer to his question.

'Our way is only for when all else fails, Mr Steele!' she snarled at him when he had the back of his head to her again. 'I am not payin' you a thousand dollars simply to act as a guide.'

Her dominant feeling was of fear now. She had to work up the anger as a thin, easily penetrable shield.

'Fine,' Steele told her. 'Here's what we do.'

As he gave instructions, he continued to follow the progress of the four horsemen as they galloped their mounts up off level ground and on to the slope. The incline forced a slackening of pace and as the dust diminished he received a clearer impression of them. And was able to pick out the source of the constant sun flashes – the metal badges which three of the men wore on their shirt fronts. Then, a moment after he realised these three were lawmen, he recognised the fourth.

The thud of hooves could be heard now and when Steele looked again into the defile behind him he saw that Mrs Lucifer was no longer pretending to hide her fear. Her fleshy features pleaded with the Virginian to announce that there was nothing to be anxious about.

'The law,' he replied.

She expelled a sigh of relief and began to show a smile.

'With Sally Swenson's Pa along,' he added.

The half-formed smile froze for a full second, then was gone: to be replaced by an expression of grim determination. 'I gave the girl my word! Please proceed, Mr Steele.'

'But no shooting!' he ordered, raising his voice. 'Unless I fire first. If there is, count me out and pay me off!'

The Concord was already rolling, the team responding to the flick of reins against their backs. It moved at the same steady pace as before the halt, but now the blinds had been pulled down at every window: just as they had been when the Apache renegades closed in.

Steele heeled his gelding forward, holding the reins in a loose grip between his palms and the saddlehorn. The riders were less than half a mile away now, and slowed their mounts to a canter when they saw the Virginian starting down the slope.

'That's him!' Swenson yelled, and almost toppled off his horse when he raised a hand to point ahead. He righted himself. 'Didn't I tell you, that's him!'

There was high excitement in his voice, and then a grin of triumph was spread across his sweat-run, dust-streaked face.

Steele showed no response as he continued to move towards the approaching riders, aware that Swenson's joy was caused by the appearance of the Concord around the rock outcrop.

One of the lawmen swung his head from side to side, to growl a word to the riders flanking him. Then all three hauled on reins to bring their sweat-lathered horses to a rearing, dust-raising stop. Swenson was taken by surprise, unable to halt his mount until he was much closer to Steele. And for a second time his squat form almost fell from the saddle as he brought his mount to a panicked, jerky standstill.

'Watch the sneaky bastard, sheriff!' Swenson yelled. 'Like I told you, he's . . . '

'Yeah, Mr Swenson,' the shortest and oldest of the trio of lawmen cut in wearily. 'I ain't forgot what you said.'

All three were accomplished horsemen, and had been able to slide Colts from their holsters in the same series of actions which stalled their mounts. They aimed them steadily now at Steele as the Virginian closed to within six feet of Swenson before reining in the gelding. Behind him, Mrs Lucifer yelled the team to a halt.

'You're Adam Steele, right?' the senior man drawled as Swenson wheeled his horse to align himself again with the sheriff and two deputies. 'The muscle for that bunch of whores on wheels.'

He nodded towards the Concord as his use of the prohibited word produced an angry snort from Mrs Lucifer.

'You've got the name right, feller,' the Virginian confirmed.

The sun-burnished, leanly built, thickly moustached sheriff had already transferred his steady gaze to the madam. 'You go by the name of Mrs Lucifer?'

'I am known professionally so,' came the thin-lipped reply.

The two deputies were about thirty, with broad builds and regular, clean-shaven features. They looked hot and weary from a long ride and kept licking their lips: from thirst rather than nervousness. Both had dull, unintelligent eyes and a hint of viciousness in the set of their mouths.

'You ain't disputin' that you got whores aboard the rig, ma'am?' the sheriff insisted, his tone still a lazy drawl.

'I most certainly am, sir! Whoever accused Satan's Daughters of being that is guilty of a grave slander and I . . . '

'Orin,' the sheriff interrupted. 'Phil. Go spill 'em outta there.'

The two deputies made to swing down from their saddles.

'You have a good reason for this, feller?' Steele asked evenly, expression neutral and sitting his horse in a composed way.

The sheriff sighed and ran the forefinger of his free hand along his moustache. 'Soon as you folks came around that outcrop, you were on the soil of my county. Now, if you just had whores with you, that'd be all right. This county ain't got no ordinances against whores, plain and simply. But Swenson here, he claims you procured his under-age daughter with intent to force her into lewd practices. And we got an ordinance against that.'

The pair of deputies had held their ground beside the horses while the sheriff drawled the explanation. Now he nodded to them and they advanced on the Concord: confidently at first, but then nervously with their Colts aimed when they saw the blinds pulled behind the shattered windows.

Mrs Lucifer was silently belligerent, glaring down at the men from high on the box seat. Steele continued to be relaxed. Swenson was breathing fast, red-faced with excitement. The sheriff appeared wearily disinterested in what was happening in front of him.

Orin went to one side of the Concord and Phil to the other.

They halted ten feet away from the two doors.

'Okay, ladies!' the sheriff called, a sudden hardness in his tone. 'You step down outta there. Ain't nothin' to be afraid of. Just want for the complainant to identify his little girl.'

'Then what, sheriff?' Mrs Lucifer demanded.

'Then I'll take you all to the county seat and lock you up until the circuit judge comes to town, folks.'

'That won't be necessary, sheriff,' Swenson put in hurriedly, his wide-eyed stare still fixed on the stalled Concord. 'So long as I get my little girl back, I'll be happy to drop the charge.'

'No skin off my nose, mister,' the senior lawman growled. 'But me and my boys didn't ride our butts off gettin' out here just to arrange a friggin' family reunion.'

'We sure enough didn't, Clem!' Orin agreed huskily, moving in on the Concord. 'And this guy said we could do whatever the hell we liked with the women, didn't he?'

Phil advanced on the opposite door. 'Come on out, girls! We're sure lookin' forward to havin' the pleasure of your company.'

Steele saw Swenson was suddenly afraid. And that it was the three lawmen who were harbouring mounting excitement at the prospect of seeing the women emerge from the coach.

'Do it, girls!' the sheriff augmented. 'Move your asses outta there to where we can see 'em. You won't have to do anythin' you ain't done before. Hundreds of times.' He laughed. 'Only difference is, you'll have to pay for our pleasure. Legal fines, that is.'

Orin and Phil had used the elder lawman's words as cover to reach the doors of the coach. As he laughed again, they fisted the handles, turned them and jerked the doors open. Their gun hands thrust the cocked Colts into the interior, suddenly flooded with sunlight.

'It's friggin' empty!' Phil snarled, as the man opposite him vented a croaked cry of surprise.

'It's a trick!' Swenson shrieked as the angry eyes of all three lawmen swung towards him. Then he raised a shaking hand and stabbed an extended finger towards the Virginian. 'I told you! I warned you he's a sneaky bastard!'

Steele had moved his right hand off the saddlehorn while the attention of all the men was directed towards the Concord. But he had sensed many pairs of eyes watching him as he lowered the hand and began to scratch at his leg, just above where the split seam gaped. One of the nervously eager watchers was Mrs Lucifer, whose own hand rested on the seat, an inch away from a Colt revolver concealed by the folds of her gown. The others were out of sight: the five whores and the runaway daughter. Crouched behind the sun-bleached rock of the outcrop with the firepower of Winchester rifles in their hands.

Steele saw the gleaming metal star on the sheriff's chest and an image of Jim Bishop flashed across the forefront of his mind. But then he thrust memories of the past away from him as he saw one lawman's Colt swing to cover him and sensed that two others were tracking on to the same target.

'What'd you do with . . . ' the sheriff started, sexual frustration powering his rage.

'Lookin' for us, fellers?' Nancy Maguire yelled, stepping into view at the side of the outcrop.

She was two hundred feet away and looking down on the stalled Concord and the men and horses close to it. Over such a distance the sheriff and two deputies could see only that she was a woman. Her features were indistinct and the shapeless dress concealed the lines of her body. But she captured their attention. And she and the others held it as Nancy started down the slope, to be followed by Hope, Gertrude, Charity and Faith. They walked with a hip-swaying gait, their hands behind their backs.

'I told you!' Swenson rasped. 'Didn't I tell you? But where's Sally?'

His relief at seeing Satan's Daughters was immediately followed by concern: as the women broke from single file into a line of advance – without Sally among them.

The women were smiling, tossing their heads to cause their red hair to swing across their faces: which helped to detract from the basic unattractiveness of their unpainted features bathed in the harsh sunlight.

Steele watched the sheriff, unable to see the expressions of the deputies since they had turned their backs on him to see the women approach. The oldest lawman had been surprised by the shout, then suspicious of the whole line of women as they appeared from behind the outcrop. Next irritated by Swenson's voice, which he silenced with a gesture of his free hand. Wary again.

'Bring your hands out in front of you!' he bellowed.

'Sure thing,' Nancy responded, and did as ordered.

The others imitated her, to reveal that they were concealing nothing behind their backs.

'Sally!' Swenson warned.

But was too late.

A rifle cracked, a sharp but distant sound. And Orin died as the report reached the ears of those who survived. He died of a clean shot in the heart, stumbling backwards under the impact of the bullet and failing to fasten a grip on the open door of the Concord.

The five whores had hurled themselves to the ground, reaching it and flattening their bodies to the dusty surface just before Orin fell, showing his stained shirt front to the disinterested sky.

Steele's knife was spinning through the dry heat of afternoon by then, drawn from the boot sheath and powered by a forceful underarm throw as he leaned sideways from the saddle.

'Sonofabitch!' Phil roared, lunging for the cover of the Concord's open doorway.

The blade of the Virginian's knife sank half its length into the neck of the sheriff's horse. The animal reared, venting a snort of pain. Its rider cursed as his aim was spoiled and the Colt loosed a bullet high into the air above Mrs Lucifer's head.

The madam screamed and exploded a shot. The bullet burrowed into the chest of the rearing horse. Two more guns exploded. A rifle bullet from the side of the outcrop glanced off the rim of a wheel close to where Phil had been standing a moment before. While his own shot smashed through the rotting timber of the Concord's construction to bury lead in the fleshy buttock of Mrs Lucifer.

Steele hit the ground with his shoulder as Mrs Lucifer

screamed for the second time. The impact jarred every bone in his body, but his hands retained their firm grip on the Colt Hartford he had dragged from the boot. And he forced himself into a half roll on to his belly: then angled the rifle up at a form in black silhouette against the brilliant glare of the sun.

The dying horse, down on its forelegs, had bucked to hurl the burden of the rider from its back. And the unsaddled sheriff was Steele's target. The range when he found it was no more than six feet, closing by the split-second to the dictates of gravity. It was perhaps less than five feet when a gloved finger squeezed the trigger.

The bullet tore into the man's lower belly, rifled through his intestines and shattered the bone of his spine before it exited at the back of his gunbelt. He was dead when he crashed to the ground, the impact spurting a great gush of blood from his back: the crimson droplets in ghastly contrast to the grey dust motes exploded by his corpse.

Steele heard horses bolting away from the cracking sounds and acrid smell of gunfire. And glimpsed three of them, one with a rider in the saddle, before he swung the Colt Hartford towards the Concord.

Mrs Lucifer was slumped across the seat, screaming as she clawed with blood-soaked hands at the source of her agony. Beyond the coach, which rocked and pitched as the team and the horses hitched to the rear tried to kick free of their restraints, the five whores were on their feet. And, just for a moment, Steele thought he had lost touch with grim reality again. For each woman was hiking the skirt of her dress up to her waist, revealing the whole lengths of her naked legs. Naked, except for a multicoloured garter mid-way up the right thigh.

Another rifle shot cracked across the snorting of the horses and the screams of Mrs Lucifer. Steele glanced up towards the outcrop and saw Sally Swenson there, a Winchester pressed to her shoulder. He snapped his head around and saw that her father was still clinging to the horse which was racing him out of range, the animal bolting in the wake of the panicked mounts of the deputies.

He looked back at the whores, in time to see them snatch Colt revolvers from their garters and lunge towards the bucking Concord: guns held out at arms length and blazing. The shots were fired wildly, from guns which jolted this way and that with the jogging action of the fast advance and their own recoil.

A hail of bullets thudded into the timber of the coach, ricocheted off its metalwork or missed completely to crack through empty air.

Steele cursed through clenched teeth and pressed himself hard to the ground as the law of chance rushed stray bullets close to him. But he continued to watch the running women, slipstream contouring their dresses to their bodies and flying their hair out from their heads. Their eyes gleamed and their complexions were flushed. The closer they came to the Concord, the greater were the number of hits they scored. And timber which was at first only splintered by bullets began to give way to the attack.

He pushed himself up into a low crouch, aiming the Colt Hartford at one open door of the coach as the women swung towards the opposite side. And he almost loosed off a shot as Phil appeared at the doorway. But instinctively stayed his gloved finger on the trigger when he saw the deputy had his back to him. There were patches of blood on his shirt and pants, but he still had enough strength to cling to the doorframe at either side. And to groan: 'Sonofabitch!' In surprise rather than anger.

All five women fired, aiming hurriedly through the open door and smashed windows across the coach from him. And Phil seemed to spring backwards as the impact of the bullets into his flesh wrenched his hands free of the frame. And at last he died after suffering the short-lived torture of the wounding hits scored against him inside the coach. For several bullets – perhaps five – took him in the head: blinding him, filling his mouth with bubbled blood and blasting chunks of flesh and shards of bone from his cheeks and jaw.

The Virginian caught a brief glimpse of the ghastly sight, before a spasming nervous system caused the corpse to turn in mid-air and thus thud to the ground face down.

For a few moments, the horses in the traces and those hitched to the rear of the Concord continued to kick and whinny. But then they became aware, as the acrid taint of drifting gunsmoke

102

was dissipated in the hot air, that the only other sound was a low moaning from Mrs Lucifer. And they calmed.

Steele rose to his feet and eased the hammer of the Colt Hartford to its safe position before he began to massage his bruised shoulder.

'Madam's wounded!' Hope shrieked.

The women hurled down their guns and rushed to climb up on the Concord.

'I'll survive!' she rasped between clenched teeth, and ignored the concern of the women to direct her pain-filled gaze towards the Virginian. 'I guess we're in real trouble now, Mr Steele? Killin' lawmen.'

He came erect after drawing his knife from the neck of the sheriff's dead horse. He wiped the blood off the blade on the animal's coat and replaced the weapon in the boot sheath.

'It depends,' he answered, glancing up the slope to where Sally Swenson was moving away from the rock outcrop, heavily laden with five Winchesters.

'On what?'

In the other direction, the two loose horses and Swenson and his mount were out of sight in the heat shimmer.

'Whether anyone gives a damn about them and how fast we can get out of this county.'

'You said *we*. Are you still with us, despite what happened here?' The chance that she had read it right seemed to ease her pain.

'He was goin' for his knife!' Nancy said quickly. 'That was the same thing as him startin' the shootin', we figured.'

Steele looked from her to each of the others in turn and failed to see any hint of nervousness, shock or remorse. Nor did any of the younger women express a tacit plea in support of Mrs Lucifer's entreaty. Nancy Maguire had made a statement rather than an excuse and the others were as coldly indifferent to his response as she was.

'I reckon you ladies have learned how to take care of your-selves,' he said.

Gertrude softened her expression and her tone was gentle and sincere. 'But we'd miss you if you left, Adam.'

103

He showed a wry grin. 'So it seems I've nothing to lose by staying.'

'What?' Charity asked, puzzled.

'As long as I keep my head down when you start shooting, I reckon you'll keep on missing me.'

Chapter Nine

Mrs Lucifer suffered greatly while Nancy and Gertrude dug the forty-five calibre bullet out of her right buttock. They probed for it with a knitting needle and extracted it with a pair of eyebrow tweezers, both instruments sterilised in water boiled on a small fire. Then they treated and covered the wound with salve and dressing from a medical kit.

The surgery was carried out aboard the Concord, while Steele and the other women waited outside in the blazing sun, listening to the madam's groans and choked screams and to the comforting words of those tending her. Faith, Hope and Charity sometimes winced in sympathy with the old woman's pain. But mostly they relished the enjoyment of triumph, often allowing their gazes to wander to the bullet-shattered and blood-stained corpses of the three lawmen, which were providing an unexpected feast for desert flies.

After watching them for a while, Steele decided they were not seeking a macabre boost for their sense of victory: rather were testing themselves to ensure that the mood they shared was genuine. And he recalled, briefly, how he had felt the need to put his own mind on trial in a similar manner – during the early days of war. And much more recently.

Sally Swenson paid no attention to the sounds from within the Concord, to the dead or to the living around her. She stood, a

Winchester held loosely in both hands, peering out across the heat-hazed Rio Grande valley in the direction her father had taken to escape the blasting guns. There was a quizzical expression on her youthfully pretty face. And, when she sensed the Virginian's eyes upon her and swung her head to look at him, she saw that his face also showed mild curiosity.

'Something bothering you, Mr Steele?' she asked.

'Reckon you could say I've got a money problem,' he replied as Nancy Maguire and Gertrude pushed open a door of the Concord and stepped down, wiping the sweat of heat and tension from their faces with the sleeves of their dresses.

'Money?' the girl asked, the lines of her puzzled frown deepening.

'Whether I'm being paid enough of it for the job I'm doing.'

Mrs Lucifer groaned as she raised herself to peer out of a broken window. 'Sir!' she exclaimed. 'We reached an agreement as to your fee!'

The Virginian nodded. 'That's right, ma'am. For escorting a bunch of professional . . . entertainers and a runaway daughter to Tucson.'

'Precisely, young man. And what has changed?'

'My father lied to the sheriff,' Sally said quickly. 'I'm not under age.'

'And I certainly have never encouraged her to become one of Satan's Daughters!' Mrs Lucifer augmented. 'So you can never be accused on any morals charges.'

'Just a few killings here and there,' Steele replied evenly.

'Knock it off, Adam,' Nancy Maguire growled. 'That's all a part of your trade. We helped you decide that.'

He nodded. 'I'm grateful.'

'So what's your beef?'

Another nod, this time to indicate Sally Swenson. 'My beef is that the one between her and her Pa is something more than they make out.'

The girl seemed on the verge of losing her new found hardness beneath a rising tide of her old style fear. Then shot a glance towards the pale, pain-wracked face of Mrs Lucifer framed by the glassless window.

The whores were abruptly intrigued.

'You were told the facts as I knew them, sir!' the madam said emphatically. 'Perhaps I did not convey at the outset just how fanatically Swenson is set on achievin' his aims. But recent events have shown that more plainly than words could have told.' She sucked in a deep breath, grimaced, and glowered around at the frowning women. 'Now, not long ago Mr Steele advised us to leave this country quickly. It was sound advice, even if it turns out to be the last he offers us.'

'Yeah, let's get the hell away from here,' Faith muttered, wrinkling her nose as she made a fast survey of the three dead men and the horse carcass. 'It's startin' to stink real bad.'

'What I've been saying,' Steele pointed out softly, so that only Nancy Maguire heard the words as preparations were made to leave the scene of the latest killings.

The fire was doused by Charity as Gertrude hauled herself up on to the seat to take the team reins. Then Nancy saddled one of the cowhands' horses while the rest of the women climbed aboard the Concord.

Steele was already sitting easy in his saddle and saw the concerned expressions on the faces of Mrs Lucifer and Sally Swenson as they watched Nancy swing astride the horse.

Then he heard the old woman rasp: 'Trust me, my dear,' as he rode out ahead of the rig and Gertrude let off the brake lever and flicked the reins.

Nancy took only a few moments to catch up with him and ease alongside him. Before the operation of taking the bullet out of Mrs Lucifer's flesh had started, the five whores had retrieved their discarded Colts. As he glanced at the woman beside him now, he saw the bulge of her gun where the dress fabric draped her right thigh.

'Ain't none of us stupid, Adam,' she said, without looking at him.

'Just good actresses?' he suggested. 'You sure looked surprised when I brought the subject up.'

She shook her head, but continued to look directly towards the foot of the slope. 'You got other things to learn about yourself, mister,' she said in a faintly chiding tone. 'And that's that you don't know every friggin' thing about everybody. You figured we were dumb enough to swallow that Swenson girl's story. So you figured you saw what you expected to see. Wasn't no surprise at all. We was just eager to see if she'd open up and spill what's really between her and her old man.'

Now it was Steele's turn to keep his attention directed ahead as Nancy Maguire studied him. What she saw was a hard set profile disturbed only by a single blinking of the eye.

'Thanks for not gettin' mad at me, Adam,' she said softly, after stretched seconds of silence between them.

'For what?' he countered as her words and the tone in which they were spoken neutralised the hard ball that had begun to expand in the pit of his stomach.

'I guess you could call it seein' through you.'

'To prove how smart you are?'

'I'm whore smart, is all. Or maybe just plain woman smart. But where men are concerned whores are smarter than ordinary women. The kind that flirt around and then maybe settle for one man. A whore does more than just flirt around with a lot of men.'

'Always thought they did,' the Virginian said with a wry smile.

Nancy did not accept his invitation to lightness. 'Somethin' bad happened to you a while back, Adam. You lost your touch and now you're findin' it again. Or maybe you found out somethin' about yourself you'd always been scared to admit before. And you still ain't got used to it. When a woman gets to know as many men as I have she can figure out things about them.'

'I'm impressed,' Steele said into the silence she left.

'Bullshit!'

Now he left the silence undisturbed. And she filled it.

'Deep down you didn't like it because a fancy whore can beat you at your own game of seein' what people really are behind the front they put up.'

'All right, lady. Deep down I don't like it because . . . '

'Leave it, Adam!' she cut in on him. 'You're grateful to us for givin' you a chance to straighten yourself out. And I figure I can talk for all of us when I say we owe you. Even a two-bit whore

108

don't like gettin' raped and we rate ourselves higher than that. Nobody wants to get killed. And if you hadn't been with us, most likely both things would've happened to us. So let's leave it there and talk about the Swenson girl.'

They had reached the foot of the slope now and were starting across a broad plain, featured with mesas and desert vegetation. Behind them, hungry buzzards felt it safe to swoop down from their high thermals and feed on human and horse flesh. On the other three sides of the slow-moving horses and coach, nothing stirred except the dust motes rising from beneath hooves and wheelrims. Overhead, the sun inched down to glare cruelly into the faces of Steele and Nancy Maguire and Gertrude.

When the two women saw him pull the brim of his Stetson lower over his forehead, they did the same with their hats. And Nancy accepted it as a signal to say her piece.

'We didn't have no reason not to believe her at first. But after a while we figured she was almighty scared of her old man. Too scared, it seemed. And the way she looks is all wrong. She told us him and her ran a spread single-handed like – just the two of them, that is. But she's soft, ain't she, Adam? Like she's never done a day's hard work in her life. Soft hands and pale face. And no muscles show from hard work.'

She looked at him for a sign of agreement and received a nod. 'How about her Pa?' she asked. 'We didn't get a close enough look at him back at Fort Pepper. Nor just now what with all the shootin'.'

'He looks like the same kind of liar,' the Virginian supplied.

Nancy vented a low grunt of satisfaction. And seemed to lose the thread of her thoughts for a few moments. Then: 'Course, we can't say there's anythin' strange about the way she's changed. We was all scared as hell the night you tied in with us and them cowpunchers showed up. And havin' you around did us all a power of good. If findin' out that killin' people is an easy way outta trouble is good.'

'Hell of a lot better than getting yourself killed,' Steele pointed out.

Nancy swallowed hard and then licked her lips. 'Unless the law catches up with you and makes you pay.'

He glanced at her and saw the flicker of fear constrict her throat and compress her lips. And, once again, the familiar image of Jim Bishop flashed across the forefront of his mind. 'It depends on the price the law wants, Nancy,' he told her and raised a hand to jerk the thumb back over his shoulder. 'I reckon those three would have been satisfied with a roll or two in the hay each.'

She gasped. 'You mean . . . ' Her throat constricted again to trap her voice. But she forced out the words. 'You mean you weren't goin' for your knife?'

'Don't reckon that matters, Nancy. Sally Swenson fired the first shot. And it was a real good one.'

'That's another thing, Adam. Now she ain't shakin' afraid no more, she shoots real fine.'

'And nobody's ready to ask her why yet?'

She had recovered her composure, but her mind seemed to be pondering the effects of other thoughts as she said: 'We all talked about it one night when she was asleep. A lot of nights before you joined us. After Mrs Lucifer checked through Sally's things. Wasn't nothin' she carries that tells anythin' about her. But she's almighty anxious to get to Tucson. So we figured it'd be best to wait until we reach there. On account of she could change her story to anythin' out here and we'd have no way of knowin' if it was true. Don't that make sense, Adam?'

'Maybe,' he allowed. 'If you reckon to make something more worthwhile than sense out of having her along with you.'

She nodded absently, her attitude still indicating that her mind was concerned with matters outside their conversation. But then she jerked herself out of her private thoughts. And gave them a link with the point Steele had raised. 'It had better be, mister! After she made us kill them lawmen back there.'

The Virginian misunderstood the reason for Nancy's latest burst of low-keyed anger.

'One good turn deserves another,' he told her.

'What's that supposed to mean?'

'A lesson for you. If you decide to ride with trouble, don't complain when you get involved.'

She shook her head. 'You got me wrong, mister. It ain't that

110

we killed them bothers me. It's that I lost two, maybe three screws!'

Steele realised he might have been shocked by the extent to which the woman was hardened by recent experiences. Then acknowledged the fact that he was not as a further sign that his reversion to what had once been normal for him was still progressing. And he pursed his lips in a silent sigh of resignation.

'Seems like the whole world's going crazy,' he muttered.

She continued to ride at his side for a few more miles, without speaking and apparently as content with the silence as Steele.

Then she growled: 'It's sure a lousy one!' in a delayed response to his comment. 'And too damn hot!'

She reined in her mount then, allowing the bullet-scarred Concord to pass her. At the pace Steele dictated, it was easy for her to swing from the saddle, hitch the horse with the other three at the rear, and clamber up on to the seat beside Gertrude.

Maintaining his thirty-feet lead, the Virginian was able to hear an exchange of words between Nancy Maguire and the women inside the coach without picking up even the gist of the conversation. But, when silence returned to the Concord, it had a quality of easiness. And he did not detect even an undercurrent of tension at the mid-afternoon stop to eat and to rest the horses.

The women went about their chores calmly, talking only when it was strictly necessary. And the expressions they wore suggested they were not acting for the benefit of themselves or anybody else.

Looking at them as a part of his constant watch on every feature of his immediate and distant surroundings, Steele realised that Nancy Maguire's report on her conversation with him could not, in isolation, have brought about such a radical change. Just as the subjects of their talk during the early afternoon ride had not caused the abrupt transformation in Nancy's attitude.

It was that the women, individually, had reached a point in their lives when they were forced into a time of transition. The cowhands, the Apaches, the soldiers of Fort Pepper and the trio of lawmen . . . if there had been just one violent incident, women

111

already hardened by their line of business would have survived intact. Perhaps, also, if the experiences with evil had been more widely separated by time and space they would have remained much as they had always been.

But the terror and the killing had been compressed into a brief time span: and after the latest slaughter on a slope of the San Andre Mountains, the burden of brutal experiences had weighed too heavily on the minds of Mrs Lucifer, Satan's Daughters and the enigmatic Sally Swenson.

It could have been a breaking point, at which the women were driven to some degree of dangerous madness. Or, as had in fact happened, a trigger to begin a cool re-appraisal of themselves. And a decision to build on the basic hardness of human nature rather than to surrender to the opposing side.

Riding through the heat of afternoon, and resting in the coolness of evening at the side of the Gila River Trail east of the Rio Grande, the Virginian continued to think about the change in the women and to relate this to himself.

After the constant violence between the lynching of his father and his killing of Jim Bishop, he had come close to the edge of insanity while he attempted to drink away his remorse in the cantina of a Mexican village. But then fresh evil had forced him to realise that his survival depended upon his own competence to combat it. And, in his mind now, there seemed to have been few interludes of peaceful calm until after Borderville – when he had made his long trip east to New Orleans.

Guns had blazed and blood had been spilled on the delta. Then on the Mississippi and Red Rivers. And at Rain. But only now, after sharing with this other group of women a period of concentrated violence, did he experience again the feeling of cold and complete self-assurance in his own abilities to meet anything his ruling fate should present to him.

They crossed the Rio Grande during the morning of the next day and continued to follow the Gila River Trail, passing no other travellers nor meeting any heading east. But while he remained constantly alert and poised to meet danger along every step of the way, the women aboard the Concord became complacent. They laughed and joked a great deal about the good days in Houston. And made plans for the future in Tucson, now that the Arizona town was a great deal closer than the Texas city. Mrs Lucifer's wound was healing and no longer caused her much pain as the wheels of the Concord seemed to bump into every pothole on the trail. And Sally Swenson was the most relaxed of all of them. No longer an outsider, she was accepted into the group, apparently on the strength of her bright chatter and eager willingness to take on the most routine and hardest of chores.

Or was their new mood a symptom of complacency as they neared their destination? It could have been a sign of their confidence in him to warn them when danger threatened again: at which time they would prove their transformation was fully hardened into its mould.

'Oh, my God!' Gertrude gasped and clamped her lips tight shut in an attempt to trap the vomit which rose into her throat.

There was no time to give a warning. The Rio Grande crossing was four days behind them and they were close to the border between New Mexico and Arizona Territories. In hill country again after traversing a monotonous scrub desert. The trail had been twisting and looping throughout the hot day, swinging wide to follow the longest but easiest route between high, bare rock ridges.

It was halfway along a curving, low-sided canyon that Gertrude saw a new brand of evil which erupted the bitter acid of bile into her throat. Since the Rio Grande crossing, all the women with the exception of Mrs Lucifer had taken to the saddle from time to time, as a relief from enduring the bone-jarring ride in the oven heat of the Concord.

In pairs or alone, they sometimes rode alongside Steele: or more often stayed close to the coach – discouraged by the Virginian's taciturn politeness in response to every attempt at conversation. But the full-bodied Gertrude was least dissuaded by his attitude: or perhaps the most content to share his long silences.

She had been alongside him for more than an hour now, enjoying the cool air of evening as the sun sank behind the horizon, turning red and ceasing to glare into her eyes. As undemanding of his company as he was of hers. But then they rode around the sharpest arc of the canyon's curve and saw the corpse.

The man had been dead for some time, for the blood which had spurted from his naked flesh was congealed into black crusts. Now the flies left him alone and nothing moved on or close to him. He lay in the centre of the trail, fifteen feet from the doorless entrance of a derelict way station. Disturbed dust and long dried blood stains showed that his newly dead body had been dragged out of the timber shell of the building to where it was now displayed: arms spread wide, legs splayed apart and head raised with the support of a cleft stick.

Arranged in such an attitude, the brutal torture he had suffered was plain to see. Both eyes were gouged out and his mouth was a sagged-open abyss filled with the pulp of his tongue and shards of shattered teeth. A hole had been cut in his throat to reveal his Adam's apple. But it had not stopped there and it was impossible to say whether it was one of these or another wound which had ended his agony with death. For his hands were almost hacked off at the wrists and his feet were connected to his ankles only by sinew. His genitals had been totally removed: and the ghastly mass of his heart hung out of the massive crater scooped in his chest.

The curve of the canyon wall which had concealed the mutilated corpse from the approaching riders also blocked the stench of its decomposing flesh until he was in sight.

'Hold it!' Steele yelled, an instant after the woman had voiced her hoarse reaction to the gruesome spectacle. He had reined in the gelding and drawn the Colt as she spoke. At the same time as he raked his eyes to left and right: noting that the way station and rims of the canyon walls were the only places of concealment immediately ahead and above.

He did not have to re-check what lay behind the Concord as Faith brought it to a creaking stop. Forty feet high rock walls facing each other across a hundred and fifty feet gap with no cover between them.

'Back up,' he snapped at Gertrude, using his heels and one gloved hand on the reins to wrench the gelding towards the cover of the curved cliff face. Insecure cover, for it protected him only from potential danger in the derelict way station.

'What is it?' Faith demanded as Gertrude wheeled her horse.

The woman in the saddle attempted to answer. But when she opened her mouth the only sound to emerge was a strangled scream.

'Steele?' Mrs Lucifer demanded, her head and shoulders jutting from a window of the Concord.

Gertrude tried again to speak, as her horse carried her away from the rotting corpse towards the coach. But this time she was unable to control her nausea and a torrent of vomit splashed to the ground.

The Virginian slid from his saddle and spat dusty saliva at the rock face. 'Something came up,' he muttered.

Chapter Ten

Steele pressed his back to the canyon side and tilted his head so that he could rake his unblinking gaze along both rims: searching for a movement to signify menacing life on the inanimate lines of solid rock against the empty infinity of the darkening sky. He had already thumbed back the hammer of the Colt Hartford, which he held in a loose grip – angled upwards and ready to swing on to a target. His ears strained to catch a sound that might give a part of a second's notice of sudden death.

But all movements and sounds were concentrated at the Concord: as the retching Gertrude half fell from her horse and women scrambled out of the door.

'A man!' Gertrude managed, gasping for breath. 'Dead and butchered! It's horrible! Spread out like somethin' in a meat market! The stink . . .'

The women listened in shocked silence, then snapped questions: their demands lost in the confusion of raised voices.

After a fleeting stab of irritation that their voices masked all other sounds, Steele was able to ignore the women. For he was too concerned with the meaning of the corpse to consider how wrong he had been about an apparent change in their characters. Perhaps because Gertrude had reacted just as he would have expected an ordinary woman to do in such circumstances.

He inched along the rock wall, continuing to keep watch

above: but increasingly certain that the danger lurked in the way station. Then, close to the point in the curve where the building would come into sight, he dropped to his hands and knees. An inch or so more and down on to his belly, moving now by a slow, paddling action of his elbows.

Behind him, the voices had been curtailed. And there were just small sounds of boot leather against dusty rock and the creak of the Concord's ancient timbers.

The Virginian's instinct – that part of his make-up which he termed his sixth sense – had a solid foundation on which to build the assumption that danger waited in the way station. And that neither he nor Gertrude were prime targets. For the Concord and horse riders had been sitting ducks the whole length of the canyon. And Steele and the woman had been exposed to easy shots for a full five seconds after seeing the corpse.

Now, with his hat off and just his forehead and eyes a target at the base of the rock face, he studied the building. It was forty feet away, a single storey structure backed against the cliff. Once there had been another building and a fenced corral, but the timbers of these had long since collapsed and lay rotted and sun bleached in the dust. The main building seemed only to have survived the same fate because it was buttressed against the canyon wall. For its timbers looked as brittle and warped as those spread on the ground.

And Steele showed a thin-lipped grin of satisfaction as he eased the barrel of the Colt Hartford out of cover: recalling the way in which the revolvers of the whores had smashed bullets through the ancient timber panels of the decrepit Concord.

'Yaaaaah!' Nancy Maguire yelled.

Steele's expression froze on his weathered face as he snatched himself and his rifle back into cover. And swung himself up on to his side, his back pressed to the rock.

He heard a whip crack, then saw it hit the ground as Nancy was hauled aboard the Concord. The coach was already moving, lunged into motion by the first galloping strides of the team. Nobody was up on the seat, but the reins were in somebody's control – leaning out of a window on the far side from Steele.

The door slammed behind Nancy and she became another

figure crouched at a window. And he saw their grim smiles before a cloud of dust enveloped the coach. He saw, also, the Winchester rifles jutting from the windows. For just an instant, the gun barrels and the smiles were directed towards him. Then the Concord had raced past, to swing into a tilting turn around the curve.

And a fusillade of shots exploded, the crackle of detonated powder amplified by the confines of the canyon walls. The horses of the dead cowhands, unhitched before the coach lurched forward, wheeled and bolted. Steele's gelding flared his nostrils and pricked his ears. But moved only a single foreleg to scrape at the ground.

The Virginian rolled on to his belly, then powered to his feet: and sprinted into the drifting dust trailed by the galloping team and hurtling Concord. His course was a diagonal line – out of the cover of the rock and into the shelter of the way station.

The shooting had been a short, sharp burst: curtailed as abruptly as it had begun. A waste of bullets, which had smashed through the rotten timber and doorless gap to impact against the rock which formed the rear wall. The only blood on the dirt floor was in black, dried patches to show where a man had been killed and butchered – or perhaps vice-versa.

Steele took this in at a glance then turned to look out through the doorway at the corpse: which had been further mutilated by flailing hooves and iron wheel rims. Almost cut in half and reduced to a pulp. But too long dead to bleed any more.

'We get 'em, Adam?' Nancy Maguire yelled.

The Concord had skidded to a rocking halt, raising yet another cloud of stinging dust. And several figures were running out of the flying motes, gowns billowing and hair streaming. Gun barrels gleamed crimson in the final rays of the dying sun.

He almost yelled a warning at them, but stemmed the impulse. Unless he had misjudged the situation, only one of them was in danger. And after the trouble she had caused, he decided he could risk her as bait.

So he simply thudded the stockplate of the Colt Hartford to his shoulder and angled the barrel skywards: stepping clear of the way station doorway so that he could cover both rims of the canyon.

The women saw his actions and came to a halt. All seven of them. But only six wrenched their eyes away from him to scan the meeting points of rock and sky above them.

Sally Swenson was staring at the awesomely mutilated corpse slumped on the trail. And it was impossible that she could recognise by the sight the man it once had been. Probably it was an instinct for the dreadful truth which exploded a reaction in her mind to power the shrill scream.

She lurched into a run.

Four shots cracked.

Bullets pocked the ground close to her pumping feet. But one found a less dispassionate target. The girl's scream faded and was silenced as she pitched to the ground with a dark stain blossoming on the bodice of her gown. She was fifty feet short of her objective.

In the gloom of twilight Steele had failed to spot the ledge just below the canyon rim across from the way station. And it was the muzzle flashes of a blazing revolver which enabled him to zero the Colt Hartford on to target.

But he had taken only first pressure against the trigger when Swenson sprang up from a crouch and hurled his gun downwards.

'No, please!' he cried. And thrust his arms high above his head.

The Virginian did not move a muscle: holding a rock-steady aim on the squat, quaking form of the man above him. Five women swung their guns to cover the same target. As Mrs Lucifer weaved between them, her bulk and her wound hindering speed.

'You don't know the truth!' Swenson pleaded, switching his attention between the man and the women. Then, plaintively: 'Is she dead?'

The ugly old madam was crouched beside Sally. Gently, she rolled the girl over on to her back and gazed sadly at the death mask of horror which contorted a once pretty face.

'Like you wanted her to be, mister!' Mrs Lucifer answered, coming painfully erect.

Swenson stopped trembling and lowered his arms.

'Madam?' Nancy Maguire blurted.

'He's the only one can tell about it now,' Mrs Lucifer answered wearily. 'Ain't that so, Mr Steele?'

The Virginian had already eased the hammer of the Colt Hartford to the rest and was canting the rifle to his shoulder when Mrs Lucifer looked towards him. Now he leaned a shoulder against a termite-riddled doorframe and waited patiently.

'Sure I wanted Sally dead,' the man on the ledge replied without emotion. 'Just wish I'd been able to kill her the same way I did that no-good sonofabitch.'

He gazed for a moment at the mangled body of the long dead man. And spat. But the saliva fell short of its intended target.

'My Pa wasn't nothin' special,' Charity snarled. 'But I'm sure glad he wasn't like . . . '

'Sally wasn't my real daughter,' Swenson cut in. 'Me and Helen took her in when she was just a baby. But everyone said we treated her better than most folks treat their own.'

'Except when it came time for her to marry the man she wanted!' Hope countered sourly.

'It wasn't that!' Swenson contested, abruptly anxious again as he sensed a new swell of enmity rise among the women. 'It was just the story she told. I'm no rancher. I run a dry goods business in Galveston.'

Now he looked hard at Steele, expecting an argument from him. But the Virginian stood and waited and listened.

'I heard what she'd said from a liveryman in Houston, Steele,' he continued hurriedly. 'Told him that to get his sympathy. She got it, too. And a fresh horse for nothin' after she'd run her own into the ground. Sally always was a good liar.'

'You did all right yourself, feller,' Steele called up to him. 'Back at Fort Pepper.'

'But not now. I wasn't ready to tell the truth then. On account of what was between me and Sally was personal.'

'And him, too?' The Virginian nodded towards the pulpy wreckage that had once been a man.

'Damn right! That's a sonofabitch named Zeke Fox, mister! And he killed my Helen for a lousy thirty-seven bucks!'

Full night had come to the New Mexico-Arizona border now. And a high, bright moon was shining: gleaming on the rock walls of the canyon and showing clearly the expressions on every face. Steele was impassive, the women were shocked and the man up on the ledge was suffering intense agony because of his bad memories.

'He near blew her in half with a scatter gun a year ago last Thursday,' Swenson went on forcefully. 'Just for the thirty-seven dollars in the cash drawer, while Helen was tendin' the store on her own.' Then he moderated his tone. 'We never did know at the time who killed her. Never suspected Fox, that's for sure. Even though everyone knew he was a no-good sonofabitch. We figured it was some drifter just passin' through town.'

The women's shock had gone now and they listened to Swenson with rapt attention: convinced of the truth they were hearing.

'Maybe I never would have found out it was him. 'Cept that Sally told me.'

'You mean . . . ' Mrs Lucifer started.

'That part of her story was true,' Swenson confirmed. 'That she was headin' for Tucson to meet up with him and marry him.' He sighed. 'Was I stupid! I knew he'd left town a couple of weeks before, but I never even knew him and Sally had ever passed the time of day together. Until I caught her sneakin' outta the house late at night with her valise.'

Gertrude gasped. 'And she just up and told you she was gonna marry the feller that killed your wife, Mr Swenson?'

He sighed again. 'You must've noticed Sally was a highly-strung girl, miss. And you've sure seen I've got a bad temper.'

Mrs Lucifer glanced at the remains of Zeke Fox and sniffed. Then wrinkled her nose as she caught a stronger scent of old death. 'There is no denyin' that, sir!'

'We had a bad fight and I hit her. Then I locked her in her room because I was scared I might hit her again. Too hard. And

121

I told her what everyone around Galveston knew about Zeke Fox. Me especially. But she knew it all herself. She got hysterical then and yelled that she knew somethin' about him nobody else did.'

Swenson paused, a mixed expression of misery and anger on his moonlit face as he recalled the night at his Galveston house. Then: 'I came close to killin' her then. Specially when she yelled at me that Fox had taken her drinkin' with the thirty-seven dollars he stole. Maybe I would've, if it hadn't been for the locked door between us. Instead, I just sat and thought out how to handle things. I sat for a long time and got nowhere. She'd got out through a window by then, and that's what decided me.'

For stretched seconds he withdrew into the private world of his memories.

'Well, I guess that's it,' Nancy Maguire said wearily, and the other whores copied her action of lowering her Winchester. 'There ain't nothin' in this for us. We always knew she was some kinda bitch, didn't we?'

'Swenson!' Steele called.

'Yeah.'

'You said you especially knew about Zeke Fox.'

He nodded. 'On account of I wasn't only keepin' a dry goods store in Galveston. I was chief of police as well.'

'Wow!' Faith exclaimed.

'He was always in law trouble but we could never prove anythin' against him.'

'You got us in law trouble, feller,' the Virginian reminded.

The squat Swenson was drained of all emotional responses now. All he could do was shrug as he said: 'I never counted on anyone except Sally and Zeke Fox gettin' killed, Steele. Her first, then him. But after I saw you in action at Fort Pepper – and found out what kind of women these were – well, I figured I'd have to . . .'

'Were they peace officers, feller?' Steele asked evenly.

'No, sir. Just three drifters I hired to wear Galveston badges and say the words I told them. I just didn't figure you'd fight the law. And that I'd be able to get to Sally without . . . But it didn't work. So I figured this out.' He spread both hands to encompass

122

the scene in the canyon below the ledge. 'I rode like hell for Tucson and used my Galveston credentials to have the local sheriff arrest Fox. Then I brought him back to this place and did what I had to do. And waited. Hopeful I might get a clear shot at Sally. Didn't care much if I lived or died. Just so long as she was dead before me.'

There was a long silence during which nobody moved: almost as if everyone was waiting for some outside influence to pronounce a verdict on what Swenson had said. But no voice spoke until Mrs Lucifer accused:

'You have been a fool, sir! If you had . . .'

'He knows that, ma'am,' the Virginian interrupted evenly, stepping away from the doorframe. He whistled softly and his gelding trotted around the curve of the canyon wall. As he waited for the horse, he tucked the Colt Hartford under an arm and drew off the buckskin gloves. 'Every man's a fool where women are concerned.'

'And women?' Nancy Maguire posed as she watched Steele swing up into his saddle, then turned to pull his crumpled jacket out of his bedroll and shrug into it.

'I reckon some of them learn by their mistakes. Some of the time. Same as men.'

'I can go?' Swenson shouted down.

The Virginian glanced up at the man on the ledge, and pushed the well-worn gloves into a pocket of his jacket. Then slid the rifle into the boot. 'Buzzards will take care of the mess you're leaving behind, feller. The one you've made of your life you'll have to clear up for yourself.'

Swenson scrambled up on to the canyon rim and went from sight. A few seconds later they heard the beat of hooves as he rode away fast. Perhaps with a destination in mind. Or maybe simply running from something rather than to somewhere.

Like Adam Steele?

'You won't be escortin' us the rest of the way to Tucson, young man?' Mrs Lucifer asked, sadly rather than anxiously.

'No, ma'am.'

'You figure we've learned from our mistakes, uh?' Nancy suggested.

He looked into her hard, whore's face. Then at each of the other younger women in turn. And suddenly realised that he had never – and still did not – differentiate between them as individuals: and that this went beyond the basic common denominator of their red hair. For, without looking at the dead Sally Swenson or the ugly old madam, he could not visualise their faces. It was as if all the women had merely been a cypher – a single entity which had influenced him and therefore had served its purpose.

'Maybe,' he allowed. 'Until you forget and make them all over again. Then you'll either pay for them or not.'

'Dependin' on the law of averages, uh?' Nancy asked.

'Talkin' of pay,' Mrs Lucifer said quickly as Steele heeled his horse forward. 'How much do I owe you?'

'Your lives,' he answered. 'But I reckon that makes us even. So let's just mark it . . .

'. . . ACCOUNT CLOSED.'*

* But another account of Steele's violent life will be published shortly.

The George G. Gilman
Appreciation Society

PLEASE NOTE *that*
THE GEORGE G. GILMAN
APPRECIATION SOCIETY
will now be operating from
Mr MICHAEL STOTTER,
42 Halstead Road, London, E.11. 2AZ.

ADAM STEELE:
THE VIOLENT PEACE

by George G. Gilman

In this fast-moving story of high adventure and daring,
Adam Steele sets out on a mission with a deadly purpose.
A vendetta that will turn old friends into enemies, and
bring a slow or sudden death to the marked men.

Abraham Lincoln is assassinated whilst at the theatre in
Washington. A great and honourable president is mourned
by many, but his passing brings rejoicing to those
Southerners defeated in the Civil War. Meanwhile Adam
Steele finds he has a private grief to mourn, when he
discovers the body of his father slowly swinging on a
makeshift gallows. This is a sorrow he cannot share with
other men. He is determined to have his revenge and sets
out on a trail of blood and violence.

On sale at newsagents and booksellers everywhere.

NEW ENGLISH LIBRARY

ADAM STEELE: VALLEY OF BLOOD
by George G. Gilman

An action-packed western featuring Adam Steele in a tale of blood and revenge. In the fourth volume of this new western series from George G. Gilman, the author of the best-selling EDGE, Steele comes face to face with a man he can only hate and despise, a man whose insatiable greed leads him to terrorise the lives of innocent people. Only Steele's split second timing and his cold nerve make death pass him by, and achieve his aim – to destroy Chance.

On sale at booksellers and newsagents everywhere.

NEW ENGLISH LIBRARY

NEL

21

YEARS

BESTSELLERS

T035 794	HOW GREEN WAS MY VALLEY	*Richard Llewellyn*	95p
T039 560	I BOUGHT A MOUNTAIN	*Thomas Firbank*	90p
T033 988	IN TEETH OF THE EVIDENCE	*Dorothy L. Sayers*	90p
T040 755	THE KING MUST DIE	*Macy Renault*	85p
T038 149	THE CARPETBAGGERS	*Harold Robbins*	£1.50
T040 917	TO SIR WITH LOVE	*E. R. Braithwaite*	75p
T041 719	HOW TO LIVE WITH A NEUROTIC DOG	*Stephen Baker*	75p
T040 925	THE PRIZE	*Irving Wallace*	£1.60
T034 755	THE CITADEL	*A. J. Cronin*	£1.10
T034 674	STRANGER IN STRANGE LAND	*Robert Heinlein*	£1.20
T037 673	BABY & CHILD CARE	*Dr Benjamin Spock*	£1.50
T037 053	79 PARK AVENUE	*Harold Robbins*	£1.25
T035 697	DUNE	*Frank Herbert*	£1.25
T035 832	THE MOON IS A HARSH MISTRESS	*Robert Heinlein*	£1.00
T040 933	THE SEVEN MINUTES	*Irving Wallace*	£1.50
T038 130	THE INHERITORS	*Harold Robbins*	£1.25
T035 689	RICH MAN POOR MAN	*Irwin Shaw*	£1.50
T037 134	EDGE 27: DEATH DRIVE	*George Gilman*	75p
T037 541	DEVIL'S GUARD	*Robert Elford*	£1.25
T038 386	THE RATS	*James Herbert*	75p
T030 342	CARRIE	*Stephen King*	75p
T033 759	THE FOG	*James Herbert*	80p
T033 740	THE MIXED BLESSING	*Helen von Slyke*	£1.25
T037 061	BLOOD AND MONEY	*Thomas Thomson*	£1.50

NEL P.O. BOX 11, FALMOUTH TR10 9EN, CORNWALL.

U.K. Customers: Please allow 22p for the first book plus 10p per copy for each additional book ordered to a maximum charge of 82p.

B.F.P.O. & Eire: Please allow 22p for the first book plus 10p per copy for the next 6 books thereafter 4p per book.

Overseas Customers: Please allow 30p for the first book plus 10p per copy for each additional book.

Name ....

Address ....

....

Title ....

While every effort is made to keep prices low, it is sometimes necessary to increase prices at short notice. New English Library reserve the right to show on covers and charge new retail prices which may differ from those advertised in the text or elsewhere.